The Inspiring Mind of a Quixotic Girl

By: C.M. Frank

For Christopher, Fallon, Slade, and Aspen,

my inspiration, my why,

with all of my love, always and forever.

A special expression of gratitude for

Mom, Dad, Joe B, Molly, and Tom

Chapter One

There I lay, on the cold tile floor of the bathroom, staring up through the skylight at the full moon staring back at me. I felt hot tears begin to form tiny puddles in my eyes, *don't do it*, I told myself, *this is exactly what she wants you to do, she wants to break your spirit, don't you dare let her*. At that moment, I desperately needed to bathe in the moonlight, I needed to feel the moon's energy pour over me. I needed to feel the moon's comfort wrap around my naked body. "Selene, give me strength", I whispered again and again as the tiny puddles ran like raging rivers down my cheeks. I was begging the moon goddess to help me reconstruct my spirit, as she had so many times before. It seemed as if she was the only person that I could talk to. Lord knows I wasn't allowed to have any actual friends. Oh no, my mother would never allow that, it would be too risky. They might actually be able to see behind the perfectly beautiful velvet curtain that she had drawn around our lives. Heaven forbid someone would see her as the neurotic woman that she actually was, instead of the perfectly polished, "good Christian", country club member that she had every bored housewife in Orleans Parish believing that she was. As strange as it may seem, I considered our maid, Neely, as my best friend. She did have to obey my mother's wishes, but I think she truly felt for me. I could see in the golden specks, within her dark brown eyes that she understood my struggle. That she wished she could take me away from this mansion, full of passive-aggressive judgment. I was forced to live in this cage after my mother had my wings clipped, at least for the time being. The moon was currently my only shoulder to cry on, as Neely had not been upstairs to witness what had occurred just moments earlier. I needed the moon, and I somehow felt, deep within my bones, that I was special, an intricate part of the universe, and on some level, however miniscule it may be, I felt that Selene, the moon goddess, truly needed me too.

A soft knock on the bathroom door interrupted my thoughts. I quickly jumped up, attempting to brush the freshly cut hair off of my body, but it was clinging to me, as if to say that it was sorry that my mother had cut it off and that it would miss me. I spotted my white terry cloth robe next to the porcelain claw-footed tub. The robe was just lying there, ever so casually, as if it hadn't a care in the world. Oh to be that robe, for just a day. The robe didn't have a mother. It had the advantage of being an inanimate object. The advantage of having absolutely no ability to feel.

"Miss Bliss, you okay, honey?" The voice of my mother's maid, Neely, muted by the solid oak bathroom door. "Yes, Neely, I'm just, ah, I just, need a minute." I stammered as I shook the robe out, attempting to get the long golden strands off of it. I began to feel the hot puddles form in my eyes once again, as I glanced around the bathroom at the clumps of hair that had graced my head just minutes before.

Tasting the stomach acid creeping up my throat, I quickly swallowed, trying to keep from losing my supper all over the black and white tiles beneath my feet. I respected the hell out of Neely, and I wasn't going to allow myself to regurgitate all of the hard work she had put into preparing that meal for me. Not on account of my mother's craziness.

"Okay, Bliss sweetie, but your momma asked me to fetch ya, she wants ya to go on to bed now. Is everything okay, baby?" she added. "I just need a minute, Neely", I replied, through the hot tears and the heat surging up my throat. Why did everything in the entire state of Louisiana have to always be so damn hot? It might make it easier to hold back tears if they didn't constantly feel like they were about to boil my eyeballs. *Shut up, Bliss, I thought. You better wash your mouth out with soap for thinking negative thoughts about living in Louisiana.* I quickly glanced through the skylight, "I didn't mean it, I promise", I whispered to the moon.

At least Louisiana had given me the honor of crowning me Miss Teen Louisiana three days prior. I was elated when I won the title, it was completely unexpected. Let me rephrase that, I was elated for approximately one-tenth of a second before I allowed my joy to be stripped from me by my mother's reaction. Why did I let her have that power over me? I longed to be able to live without abandon, being able to be the person that the good Lord had created me to become. If Cecily Fontaine had anything to say about it, I would be trapped here in this sheltered world within the confines of this house until I withered away. My certificate of death would read; "Bliss Marie Fontaine, cause of death, lack of creative stimulation and suffocation of spirit."

***

My mother had entered me into the pageant circuit last year because all of her hoity-toity friends at Magnolia Country Club had been boasting about their daughters and step-daughters entering the local, Miss Teen New Orleans pageant. Of course, my mother, not to be out done, decided that I would enter the pageant as well. When she told me that I would be entering, yes she *told* me, she did not *ask* me, as any other mother in a civilized society would do, I just politely nodded. Of course, I knew that her motive for entering me into the pageant was most certainly a selfish motive, but I agreed, nonetheless. It's called saving your ass, a technique of which I mastered years ago. When you have been Cecily Fontaine's daughter for seventeen years, you learn a thing or two about the inner workings of a deeply disturbed and conceited mind.

I was actually looking forward to being in the pageant because that meant I would have the opportunity to step out of my sheltered, heavily controlled homeschooled life, if even for one evening. *I could actually make friends with my fellow contestants. Maybe momma will be okay with it, just this once, since she is friends at the club with half of their mothers*, I thought. My puppet master of a mother actually put her strings down and let me be myself and talk to the other contestants. I ended up winning the title of Miss Teen New Orleans and was invited to participate the next month in the Miss Teen Louisiana pageant. I was beyond giddy. I felt proud and it seemed that I had made my mother proud of me as well.

In the weeks leading up to the big statewide pageant, she bought me a new dress, new shoes, new makeup, the whole nine yards. Of course, from what I had seen on TV, most mothers, who actually wanted a *real* relationship with their daughter, would invite their daughter to go shopping with them for all of these things. Of course, my point of reference was drawn from fictional characters, created by clever writers who knew how to tug on the audience's heartstrings. I wasn't entirely sure that anyone had that much cohesiveness in their relationship with their mother, but nonetheless, I envied them. Don't get me wrong, I was pleased that my mother thought enough of me to get me the dress, the shoes, and the makeup, but I wished that she craved having that bonding experience the way that I craved it.

The four weeks passed very quickly, and before I knew it, the Miss Teen Louisiana pageant was upon me. I felt poised and ready as I took the stage. A surge of confidence coursed through my veins, this was a feeling that was unfamiliar to me. I had never felt confident in the entire seventeen and a half years that I had been on this earth. I wasn't allowed to feel good about myself. I could feel myself exuding a proud energy on that stage. It felt as if I was caught up in a whirlwind. The evening passed very quickly, which then brought upon us the crowning moment.

"Your 2000, Miss Teen Louisiana is…", the crowd waited with baited breath, as the tuxedo clad, spray tanned, hairpiece wearing, Master of Ceremonies continued, "Miss Teen New Orleans, Bliss Fontaine!". Once my name was announced, I looked into the crowd at my mother's face. I foolishly expected her to beam back at me with pride. Instead I looked down at a woman that had disgust and hatred strewn across her face. She was jealous of the attention that this was bringing to me. Why did I think she would be any different? Why did I let my guard down? I shouldn't have agreed to be in the pageant. *This wasn't my idea!* I wanted to scream at her. *It was your idea!* Why did I have to actually try to win? Didn't I realize that winning would escalate her neurotic fits at home?

During that moment, my crowning moment, what should have been a proud moment in my life, one that I could share with my children and grand children one day, everything began to move in slow motion. I do not remember the crown being placed on my head, nor do I recollect posing for photographs afterwards. My mind and body became completely consumed with what her face conveyed. Perhaps this was my body's defense mechanism, becoming numb to the situation at hand. It was as if I subconsciously shut down in order to shield myself from harm or heartache.

***

My subconscious was in full defense mode once again as I stood in the moonlit bathroom. I might as well have been a defensive lineman for the New Orleans Saints. I was that serious about my defensiveness. I had to be, it was the only way I could survive in this house, without turning into a full on bipolar mess, like my momma. I shook my head quickly, trying to wake myself from the flashback, the horrid pageant flashback. That was the evening that had propelled my mother into her "souped up crazy mode", as I called it. Winning the pageant caused the Edward-Scissorhands-on-crack haircut. The haircut that my mother had so graciously given me, just minutes before.

"You think you're just the prettiest girl in all of Louisiana, don't you," my mother had screamed as she chopped chunks of golden locks off of my head. "You think you're better than everyone else, you think you're so smart and clever. You wouldn't be anything without me," she screamed, "Let's see how gorgeous you are now", she hissed into my ear. I stood there, stoic, as she chopped away at my hair and at my dignity. This was her form of punishing me. I had learned it was better to just stand there and take it. *She will leave in a minute, she will come to her senses, feel guilty and leave the room. Then you can cry,* I thought to myself. *Do not cry in front of her. Do not let her see that she gets to you. Be strong.* Once my oppressor decided she had done all of the damage that she could at that particular time, she took her leave. It took me a moment to transport myself back into reality from the comfort of the astral plane that I had allowed my mind to drift into once again. Allowing my mind to check out from reality was an exhausting process. I slowly slunk down to the tile floor, reluctantly regaining full consciousness into the palpable reality and draining heaviness of the moment.

A cold chill tickled my spine, despite the warmth of that April evening. Goose bumps began to pop up on my arms, although my body was adorned with the thick terry cloth robe, which I wrapped tightly, hoping it would lend comfort in my time of need. I turned my gaze to the bathroom mirror. My soft long hair was gone. The vision staring back at me through the beautifully ornate oval mirror, was a completely foreign portrayal of myself. *You have truly out done yourself this time, Cecily Fontaine,* I thought. My mother had always been "creative" with the punishments that she bestowed upon me, but she had gone above and beyond with this one. *Does Virginia Woolf know about you, Momma? I think even she would be jealous of how insane this is,* I thought.

There I stood with a chopped up mess on my head. It looked as if I had gotten into an argument with a weed-eater and it had emerged victorious. I swear, I looked as if I belonged in a mental institution. I half expected the paddy wagon to pull up in front of the house, ready to take me away and lock me up in a padded-wall prison. "No, no," I would say, "I'm not the crazy one, she is!" "You've got the wrong girl, my mother is the one you want, not me," I would yell, as they drug me out of the door kicking and screaming. What a riot that would be! I would not be surprised if people thought that I was the psycho. With this botched haircut, who could blame them? This was my mother's twisted way of punishing me for succeeding in something. She could not put her ego aside and let me have one glorious moment. *She hates me this much,* I thought. *She wants to humiliate me, this is her way of proving that she has control.* I cannot believe that I did not foresee something like this when I agreed to participate in the pageant.

My mother's wrath was relentless. I knew that if I stalled much longer, she would unleash yet another one of her many imaginative penalties upon me. Neely had already knocked several times, and heaven knows my mother is not a patient woman. Therefore, as a defensive measure, I knew that I should emerge from the solace of the bathroom and face my foe.

Chapter Two

My father was not a perfect man. My memories of him are blurred remnants, due to the fact that he walked out of my life when I was four years old. My mother would not allow me to speak his name or ask any questions about him. The rough mosaic of the story that I had was constructed from tid-bits of information that I would gather from Neely. My interpretation of the events that led up to my father's disappearance from our lives was rather askew and greatly lacking in detail. I wasn't fully convinced that the miniscule amount of details that I had managed to get out of Neely weren't tainted cognition. Cecily Fontaine was a master manipulator, always tipping the scales in her favor. She may very well have brainwashed Neely into believing her delusional reality, for all I knew.

As a young child, I made a game of gathering clues to piece together. Neely began playfully referring to me as, "Detective Bliss Fontaine, the sweetest sleuth this side of the Mississippi". I would giggle and modify her reference by telling her that I was "the sweetest sleuth in all of the land", not just this side of the Mississippi. That was when I was still self-assured, prior to the thirteen year confidence beat-down that I had endured from Ms. Cecily Fontaine herself, the most deranged and disturbed narcissist in all of the land.

Judging by the evidence that I gathered from Neely, my mother was not completely to blame for her faults. My father had been a highly esteemed and well compensated business man, hence the lavish late 1800s antebellum mansion that my mother and I lived in. My parents had purchased the home in 1978, four years prior to my arrival. It was the only home that I had ever known.

Along with my father's executive position came stress and pressure, which Neely claimed, turned my father into an "abusive mess of a man". Apparently he would come home from his office and take his frustrations out on his wife. Neely said it began with him yelling at my mother and shaking her when I was an infant. It escalated into open-handed slaps across her face and that he even punched her once. I often asked Neely why my mother would stay if things were really that bad. I didn't believe that my father had truly been that horrible, I felt that this was probably part of an embellishment that my mother had force-fed to Neely. I could just imagine my mother saying to poor Neely, "You better tell Bliss that he was the devil incarnate. Make me look like the innocent victim, like I am an angel. Don't you dare make me look bad. Make her hate his guts!"

I wasn't convinced of the accuracy of Neely's recollections, but the majority of the time I would politely listen and nod, as if I understood and accepted this as truth. I carried on with my sleuthing on various occasions for years. Until one day, two years ago, my sleuthing led me to find something that I wish I could erase from my memory.

Chapter Three

It was a Saturday afternoon in 1998 and my fifteen year old self was bored. My mother had gone to have tea with her friends at Magnolia Country Club and Neely was at the supermarket doing the shopping for the upcoming week. Neely always did the week's shopping on Saturday afternoons, but my mother usually waited to have tea with her friends on Sunday afternoons, after church. Neely had mentioned something about one of my momma's well-to-do friends having to leave that evening in order to visit family in London, causing the change of days. When Neely told me, I was four chapters into the book, To Kill a Mockingbird, which meant my mind belonged to Harper Lee, at least for the time being. I was wrapped up in early 1930s Alabama, when Neely's voice dissolved the temporary trance-like state that I had fallen into. "Miss Bliss Marie! I have been patient enough now, darlin', don't make me tell ya a third time. Did ya hear me or are you gonna make an old black woman repeat herself again? Guess you just think that I've got nothin' better to do" "Oh, I'm sorry, Neely. You have my full attention now," I told her. She proceeded to tell me of my mother's change of plans and that they would both be gone for the remainder of the afternoon. "Now, I'm happy to have ya as company at the market, if ya don't want to be all by yo'self," she offered. Neely was always taking my well-being into account. I loved her. I wished that she could be my mother. She was the only person in the entire world with whom my opinion mattered. "That's okay, Neely, I'll just stay here and read. Harper has me right where she wants me," I grinned at Neely as I said it. She grinned right back at me and nodded her head. "That has always been one of my favorite books too. When did you sneak in and snag that one, Miss Thing?" she inquired. Neely was smart, she loved to read. She was actually the one who taught me how to read. Two walls in her room were bookshelves stuffed with great novels. She loved to tease me about sneaking books from her room, although I knew that she liked sharing her passion for reading, adventure, and knowledge with me. It was our sacred bond. My mother wouldn't have liked it, which made it that much more appealing to me. "I'll get you some of those cherry candies that you like so much. See ya in a few hours, honey," she said, as she disappeared out of the door and out of sight.

It was strange that my mother was allowing Neely to carry on with her Saturday afternoon shopping, knowing that I was going to be left to my own devices at home all alone. Perhaps she assumed that Neely would insist that I go along with her to the market. Regardless, I knew for sure that the fact that they were both absent meant one thing, it was the perfect time to investigate. I decided to venture up into the attic to see if I could find a photograph of the man that my mother and Neely had wrongfully accused of being a complete cowardly jerk of a man. *I apologize, Scout, Jem, and Atticus, but you will have to excuse me for a bit. I have some extremely urgent business to tend to*, I thought as I grabbed the Seventeen magazine that Neely had bought for me the week before, from underneath my mattress. She was excellent at sneaking me special surprises. I quickly tore a corner of one of the pages and placed it into the book as a makeshift bookmark. Then I dashed out of my room and towards the stairwell. I didn't know how long they would be gone, and I wasn't going to waste my golden opportunity.

As I climbed the stairs, I thought, I love you Neely, but I do not like how you speak ill of my father. I do not like the impression that you have given me of him for years now. It is time for me to clear his name, once and for all. Surely he wasn't the villain, my mother was the villain. There was not one glimmer of uncertainty in my mind that he was an upstanding man. My mother probably threatened Neely within an inch of her life. She made Neely speak ill of him. It's okay Neely, I understand. I still love you, I thought. When I unveil the truth, a weight will be lifted from your shoulders as well. I'm doing this for you and me.

My head tingled as I crept quietly up the stairs to the third floor, where the attic door stood. Part of me expected my mother to be hiding somewhere in the house, trying to catch me sneaking around. I would not be surprised if the whole Saturday afternoon tea was simply a ruse formulated in order to give her a reason to punish me. This thought intensified the tingling sensation. It was as if a million tiny ants were crawling on my scalp, screaming at me in their almost inaudible voices, "No, Bliss don't go in there!" "You will be dead meat if your mother finds out you went into the attic, don't do it!" *Hush up*, I thought. *I am a girl in search of the truth and I am going to make good on my father's name. Neely and my mother better pray to Jesus that they don't go to hell for falsifying information, disgracing my father like they have. When I reveal that he was a good man, I will never speak to Neely again, I won't even be able to look at her. Yes, I realize that less than ten seconds ago, I was thinking about what a godsend Neely is. I have the right to be indecisive about my feelings on this matter. I have the right to be upset and fickle about this. It is my prerogative! I have earned the right to be weird about it, hell I've endured enough weird crap from my mom throughout my lifetime, you're damn right, I've earned my indecisiveness! I want to hold Neely in high regard, but I also don't want to think bad things about my dad. I don't want my mother to be right about him, she cannot be right about him. My mother, oh she is going to wish she had never lied to me. I will find my father and he will be so happy to see me that he will want to take me in and have me live with him. I will never have to deal with Momma again!*

The tingling sensation traveled down my arms, surged through my legs, and into my toes as I grabbed the door knob. What would I find on the other side of this door? I was forbidden to go into the attic, it had always been a house rule and I had never crossed the line. I was now in full rebel mode. I attempted to turn the knob, only to find that the door was locked! *Who the hell locks their attic door,* I thought. *She probably has voodoo dolls, shrunken heads, and bats blood hidden in there. That damn witch!* I glanced around trying to devise a plan of action, when I noticed a bronze statue in the corner near the door. I tiptoed over, bent down and attempted to lift the base of the statue. Lord, have mercy! It was heavy, but I was a girl on a mission and at the point of no return. I had to find clues as to my father's whereabouts. He would rescue me from this uppity prison that I was living in. "Get me out of this fancy Alcatraz, Daddy", I whispered.

Waifish arms, don't fail me now, I thought, as I attempted to hold the base of the statue up high enough so that I could peak underneath. As I pressed my cheek to the floor, I squinted my eyes and could faintly make out a dark object. Carefully balancing the weight in my left hand, I quickly slid my right hand underneath the statue, when I felt the outline of a key. "I knew it", I whispered, "the sleuth still has it!" I grinned, thinking that I was glad to be such a clever girl. I was proud to have kept my vivacious personality, despite the insane attempts by my mother to make me basic and boring. *I will never lose my sense of humor*, I thought. *It's one of my qualities that I treasure the most, I will not let it go down in flames.* I slid the metal key out and began to cautiously lower the statue. *Don't fall, don't fall*, I silently pleaded, looking up into the beautiful bronze face of Persephone. I was unaware that my mother owned this statue, as I had never been permitted to explore this part of the house. My countless hours of studying Greek Mythology was paying off. I was pleased with myself for recognizing Persephone. When the statue was once again safely on the ground, I grabbed the key and slowly stood up, putting me at eye level with the goddess herself. In that moment, I felt a connection with her. She would empathize with my misery. It was Persephone, after all, that had been abducted by Hades, the king of the underworld, and forced to live there as his bride. *I feel for you, girl*, I thought. *I am living in my own version of hell.*

The metal key had been tarnished and it was unusually heavy in my hand. I wasn't sure if the weight of it was oddly greater than that of most keys, or perhaps, the dense feeling was representative of years of oppression and burdens that would magically vanish upon entering the mysterious threshold of the attic. I hoped it was the latter. I *needed* to find out the truth and be rescued. I slid the key into the keyhole on the etched doorknob. *It fits! Thank you, Jesus, Mary, and Joseph,* I thought. As I turned the key to the left I heard the faint click of the lock succumbing to the power of the key. *Thank you Persephone!* I turned around, looked right at that beautiful woman and winked. If I hadn't known better, I could have sworn that she winked back.

Chapter Four

My hands trembled nervously as I attempted to gather up the courage to push open the door to the unknown. This was it. I just knew that my entire life was about to change. *Once I find clues to my daddy's whereabouts, I will plan my escape. I will whisk myself out of this psych ward so fast that half of the Garden District will choke on the dust clouds left behind my happy ass. "Sorry for the dust in y'all's Bloody Marys", I would yell with a gigantic smile on my face, as I zipped past all of my mother's bleach-blonde, fake, plastic friends.*

I pushed open the door and stepped through the threshold. All I could see were red and blue spots that seemed to float in the air. I squeezed my eyes shut, opened them, then blinked quickly three times, in an attempt to adjust to the darkness. The brilliant idea of bringing a flashlight had not occurred to me. I stretched my long, thin arms out, reaching into the spotted abyss. *There has to be a light switch somewhere in here*, I thought to myself as I cautiously took baby steps towards my left. *Now if I could just find the dang wall! Why did I not think to bring a match or something with me? You cannot screw this up Bliss, this might be the only chance you'll ever get to find some answers.* As I shuffled my feet, still unable to see a thing, I heard something scurry quickly away from me. *Holy crap, it's gotta be a filthy rat!* There was no telling how many creepy-crawlies could be lurking in this darkness, ready to gnaw my pretty face off at any given moment. Horrible thoughts of giant spiders, and blood-sucking bats were swirling through my head when my foot banged into something hard, propelling me forward. I caught myself and suddenly a sharp pain surged from my wrists up my forearms. I gasped and blinked back hot tears already welling up in my eyes. *You're okay, Bliss, suck it up.* I told myself, as I shook my arms out, making sure to breathe in deeply through my nose and out through my mouth. That was a trick that Neely taught me when I was six years old. She would say, "Now darlin', you gotta just breathe that calmin' breath and you'll be okay". Somehow she knew how to make everything alright.

Once the pain subsided a bit, I looked down to see the cause of my ever-so-graceful stumble. My eyes were now almost completely adjusted to the darkness of the attic, allowing me to make out the large, rectangular shape of a chest or a trunk of some sort. Butterflies fluttered in my stomach as I felt for the latch. Lifting the top of the trunk took almost as much strength as lifting the Persephone statue had taken. The moment the lid lifted, I smelled the most disgusting smell that I had experienced in my life. I began to dry heave. My gag reflex was unsympathetic to the fact that I was on borrowed time at the moment. I didn't have time to act like a sissy girl. Holding my breath and covering my nose and mouth with my hand, I leaned over the open chest and squinted my eyes. I could see a large lump, which appeared to be a blanket. Reaching out to touch the lump confirmed my prediction. My hands felt the softness of a comforter. *Darn, I was hoping the chest had pictures or documents within it. An old nasty comforter does me no good.* I wondered why my mother would bother to keep this old thing, Cecily Fontaine only bought the most expensive comforters with ornate stitching.

Although she did not treat me well, she still insisted that my room be decorated with the same high standards that the rest of the house had. I knew that it was not for my benefit, it was surely for the benefit of the superficial women in her social circle. They would stop by from time to time, and my mother loved to showcase her alter ego in front of her clique. "Y'all look at how sweet Bliss is, isn't she turning into such a beautiful young lady," she would ask her friends. Then, of course, the most shameless ass kisser of the group; there is always one of those; would reply through a stiff, fake excuse for a smile, "Oh, Cecily, she is a spitting image of you. You have done such a wonderful job raising her, and all on your own. I just don't know how you do it. You are super mom. I wish I could be just like you." I swear, my mother and her group of suck ups could put Sandra Bullock's acting skills to shame, the way they carried on.

I glanced around the room and saw the outline of an armoire, a roll top desk, a few lamps, a canopy bed, a dollhouse; that I could only assume was mine, prior to my dad leaving; several cardboard boxes, and two more rectangular shaped trunks. I was grateful that my eyes had finally adjusted enough to see farther than six inches in front of my face. "Hallelujah!" I whispered. I was sure that I would be able to find enough pieces to solve the puzzle. Somewhere amongst the boxes, desk, and trunks, I was sure to get the answers that I so desperately craved.

I sauntered towards the boxes, grateful to step away from the dreadful stench, and careful not to move anything. I was not willing to risk my mother finding something moved. I shivered thinking about the wrath she would bestow upon me, were she to find out that I had snooped.

I had actually never heard my mother say that she was going up into the attic at any point in my life. Knowing her, she must have thought that it was beneath her to do such a thing. Manual labor was something that she had always acted as if she was allergic to. I had heard her tell Neely to move items into the attic, or bring items down from the attic, several times. I did not need for Neely to see something shuffled around up in the attic and to bring it up to my mother. I did not want to give momma any suspicions that I had visited the attic, heck, I could not afford to do anything that might intensify her discipline techniques. I decided to make certain that I was extra careful to leave everything just as I had found it.

Dang it, I forgot to close the trunk lid! I thought, as the wretched smell permeated every last inch of fresh air in the attic. "Get it together, Bliss", I mumbled under my breath. I tiptoed back over, retracing my steps. Of course, the smell got stronger, the closer I got to the trunk. It was like a trail of breadcrumbs that refused to be ignored. *What the heck is that smell?* It was unlike anything that I had ever smelled. A thought crept into my mind; perhaps a huge rat had died in that trunk, or perhaps a whole family of huge ass rats. The thought made me shudder. As I reached out to close the lid, my subconscious could not shake the thought that keeping a dirty, disgusting comforter was completely unlike my mother. I do not remember reaching and pulling the comforter out. I swear, my spirit guides must have moved my body for me.

A blood curdling scream emanated from my body. "Holy shit, oh my God!" I yelled. I tasted the vomit in my mouth. I swiftly lifted the bottom of my t-shirt, pulling it up just in time to upchuck that afternoon's chicken salad sandwich all over the Blink 182 logo. I felt dizzy. *This cannot be real, I must be having a nightmare*, I thought. But it was real, there was no denying it. There it was. A partially decayed, human body underneath the comforter. The smell was rancid, and I had to gasp for a breath. I wanted to run out of that attic faster than Speedy Gonzales himself, but I knew that I had to look closer. I had to find out if this was who I thought it was, my father.

As I leaned closer, the stench almost made me faint. Then I saw it, barely visible through the deep red, almost brown, stain on the white collared shirt adorned by the deceased. A monogram stitched onto the pocket. Three letters. It had to be the deceased's initials. The horrid smell permeated the air and my eyes burned like somethin' fierce as I squinted them and leaned in to make out the letters. MJF, it had to be my daddy! Something, something, Fontaine. I didn't know my father's first or middle name. They had never been spoken to me in all of my fifteen years, but surely the 'F' on the monogram stood for Fontaine. It had to be him. *She killed him, my mother killed her own husband.*

I had always known that my mother was capable of inhumane deeds, but I had never expected murder to be one of them. This was much worse than anything that my imagination had envisioned to be hidden in the attic. *Did Neely know about this? Was she in on it with momma?* I shook that chilling thought from my head as I tossed the comforter back over the body of my poor father. *I hate Cecily Fontaine*, I thought, as I allowed myself to lie on the dirty floor, weeping for a man that I barely knew. I felt as if I was in a trance, shocked by my findings. I could not have told you how long I laid on the attic floor, alternating between crying uncontrollably and staring stoically at the trunk. I was forced back into reality when I heard a noise. It sounded like the shutting of a door, and it came from somewhere in the house.

I jumped up so quickly, you would have thought that a snake had bitten me. I did the sign of the cross over the open trunk and whispered, "She will pay for this, Daddy, I promise. I love you, Daddy", before I quietly closed the lid. It seemed as if each and every wooden board creaked under the weight of my feet as I snuck across the floor towards the open door. *Shut up!* I wanted to scream at the floor, but I knew there was no avoiding the squeaks and creaks within a house that was more than one hundred years old, no matter how fancy the home.

Once I reached the door, I squeezed my hand into the pocket of my denim capri pants and located the key. Sweat began to form along my hairline and down the back of my neck as I carefully closed the attic door. "Miss Bliss, I got you those candies, sugar." It was Neely, she was back. I could faintly hear her from the third floor. She must have still been on the first floor, in the kitchen, putting the groceries away. *Good, that means she hasn't gone looking for me in my room yet*, I thought. My hand trembled as I put the key into the hole and turned it. I was almost home free. I just had to get the attic key back underneath the gorgeous goddess and make my way back to my room. *Now Persephone, can you lose about twenty pounds real quick for me? Not that you're fat girl, no you are perfect, it's just that I am in kind of a rush right now. I would be forever indebted to you*, I thought as I prepared to lift her up one last time. I took a deep breath, just the way Neely had taught me, I lifted the statue and slid the key underneath it. As I stood and began to walk to the stairs, which would lead to the safety of my bedroom, I quickly turned and looked back at the Persephone statue. I raised my right pointer finger to my full lips and winked, as if to tell her that this was our special little secret.

I descended the stairs from the third floor to the second as quickly and quietly as I could. As I advanced down the long hallway, toward the comfort of my bedroom, I could hear my heart. It was beating incredibly loudly. I felt as if the volume of each beat was going to give me away. "Bliss, did you hear me, child?" Neely's voice echoed through the hallway, and I knew that she must be ascending the stairs, close to the second floor. *Just get to your bedroom, hurry up*, I said to myself. I could now hear Neely's footsteps, actually her steps were always more like a shuffle or a waddle. I always thought it was sort of funny, the way she waddled, almost like a penguin, with the weight of her rather large frame. I knew she was close to the top of the stairs by now. I had counted eleven footstep thuds, since she last called my name, and I knew there were exactly fifteen steps on the staircase that lead from the first floor to the second. *Hell, she could be at the top by now*, I thought. I assumed that when she called my name, she had already climbed a least a couple of steps. "Bliss Marie! What is wrong with you girl? Do you want your candy or not?" I turned around and saw Neely standing at the front of the hallway looking right at me. "Oh, I'm sorry Neely," I mumbled, unable to look at her. She might have been in cahoots with my mother, after all. "Goodness gracious, you poor thing! Just look at you," she exclaimed. "Go lay down and I will bring ya some ginger ale and some saltine crackers. Do ya need a cold compress too, sweet baby?" I had completely forgotten about the vomit covering my shirt. I must have looked like a hot mess. I knew that my fair skin was probably red and blotchy and that my eyes were probably puffed up, due to the sobbing I had been doing only minutes before. I knew I had to switch into Oscar nominee mode. "Yes please, Neely. I am so sick, I can barely move," I groaned. I hated lying to Neely, but once again, I had to save my own ass. I wasn't sure if she would tattle tell on me, if she knew what I had really been up to. "Okay darlin', change your clothes and get into yo' bed. I will be right back," she promised. I slogged slowly into my room. I had to make it look like I really was sick. I actually was sick, but not in the way that Neely had assumed that I was. I was sick to my stomach, sickened at the thought of my murderous mother.

I peeled off my t-shirt, carefully trying to keep the chunks of vomit from getting into my hair, which proved to be quite the daunting task, as my hair was still long and beautiful, at that point. So beautiful, it would have put Aurora from the movie, Sleeping Beauty, to shame. Never would I have imagined myself with a botched up haircut that made me look like a crazy boy. As I put on a satin nightgown and crawled into my bed, I wondered what my next move should be. *Should I call the police and tell them what I had found rotting away in our attic? That might be too risky, after all, my mother had killed once, that I knew of. It's possible that even more poor souls have lost their lives by her hand. She could do it again, and I certainly will not be her next victim. Should I run away? If I did, where would I go? My mother would make it her mission to find me, and what about Neely? She couldn't have been in on the murderous rampage and I couldn't leave her in the clutches of a psychopath.* I felt the sharp twinge of a migraine starting. *Great, that's all I need right now*, I thought sarcastically. I had been through more trauma in one afternoon than most people have to deal with in their entire lives. I took a deep calming breath and decided that I would act as if everything was normal, as if I was not wise to the reality of the situation, at least for the time being. I had to be smart about it. As difficult as it would be to face the woman who had taken my father's life and in turn, made mine a living hell, I would have to do it, in order to survive. *Yes, that's the only way I will get out of here alive*, I thought to myself, *I will have to just take my time in order to devise the best escape strategy.*

Chapter Five

Being a prisoner can have numerous different meanings, if you really think about it. Although I wasn't confined in a cell with steel bars, I was most definitely a prisoner. I had felt trapped my entire life, but that fateful trip to the attic in 1998, when I made the awful and gruesome discovery, caused a palpable angst to build up inside of me. I wasn't bitter towards life, I was bitter towards my poor excuse of a mother. I had such a tangled mix of emotions, I was sad about the horrible fate that my father had endured, I was infuriated with my momma for doing what she did, I was frustrated that I couldn't do anything about the situation, I felt imprisoned, paranoid as all get out, and you bet I was scared shitless. You try living under the same roof with a neurotic killer. I didn't sleep well for those two years. I half expected to wake up in the middle of the night to find my mother sitting in the rocking chair that was in the corner of my bedroom, rocking slowly, humming "Rockabye Baby", holding a butcher's knife, menacingly watching me sleep. Just add a few disembodied baby laughs and you've got yourself a box office thriller. I don't think my wild imagination allowed me to sleep for more than four hours at a time.

I found myself teetering between being amicable to my mother, out of fear, and having fits of rage towards her. Of course, the fits of rage existed only in my head. I knew that was the only safe place for them to be. There were many days when I wasn't sure if I would be physically able to contain my anger within the confines of my body. I felt as if all of the hate, anger, sadness, and oppression I was feeling would just burst out of me, all over my mother's Chanel suit. I was not deranged like her, I could never pull a Menendez, although being rid of Cecily Fontaine sounded pretty good to me.

My mother did not seem to notice the change in my mood and behavior, which spoke well of my self-control, as there were many evenings at the dinner table that I had to use every bit of self-restraint that I could muster, not to blurt out, "You are an evil murder and I detest you!" Most evenings we would sit and eat our supper in silence, never looking at each other. I swear, I could easily duplicate the ornate pattern on the rug that sat on the dining room floor. If you counted the numerous hours that I spent eating and staring at it, in order to avoid looking at that woman, I bet it would add up to at least a week's worth of time. Of course, Neely noticed that I had changed. "So I suppose I need to buy ya some black lipstick and some emo CDs, since you've lost all yo' sense of humor," she'd say jokingly. "I'm sorry, Neely, I'm just not feeling like myself today," I'd reply. I had my list of usual excuses. Half the time, Neely probably just assumed that Aunt Flo had visited me, and I gladly let her believe what she wanted to believe. She would make comments here and there about my moodiness, which were all in good humor, but one day, I crossed the line and she let me know it.

I had never seen Neely get angry. Yes, I'd seen her get frustrated when I wasn't paying attention during the school lessons that she was trying to teach me, or when I failed to pick up my wet towel from the bathroom floor, but I had never actually heard her raise her voice. It happened the day after my mother had cut all of my hair off, punishing me for succeeding in the pageant. I think it was the combination of the weight of the ugly temperament that I had been carrying around for two years, and the embarrassing hair that I was involuntarily sporting that caused my unusual outburst. My mother had gone to have brunch with her so-called friends at the country club.

Neely and I were seated across from each other in the study. She was going over chapter eight in my French IV textbook, "Conjugaison de Verbes", when I just could not contain myself any longer. "I thought you cared about me! How the hell could you not tell me, Neely?" I screamed. "I beg your pardon, Miss Bliss? I think you might want to check yo' self then start again with a better tone of voice, young lady.

I'm gettin' tired of your bad-ass attitude." she huffed. "Now, where were we? Hmm, let's see…elle parlerait…" she continued. "I'm talking about what happened to my father, Neely. I know she killed him. How could you stay and work for a murdering bitch?" I screamed, staring at her wrinkled, mocha colored face. Tears raced down my smooth, porcelain cheeks. They felt scorching hot on my skin. I just knew they were probably searing permanent scars onto my face. I didn't care. *My mother wants me to look ugly, fine then, I'll look ugly. But I'll never be ugly like momma, ugly on the inside, never*, I thought, as I hastily wiped my tears with the back of my hand. Neely looked up from the textbook very slowly, but when she looked into my eyes, the soft, kind, golden specks that danced within the chocolate color of her irises; the specks that I had become so fond of, the specks that had provided me comfort for as long as I could remember; those specks had vanished. Neely furrowed her brow and stood abruptly from her chair. "Child, ya don't know what you're talkin' 'bout and I suggest ya shut yo' damn mouth before ya hear somethin' that ya do not want to hear!" she yelled. It startled me to hear Neely speak so harshly to me, but I was livid and I was not going to back down. "I suppose you were in on it with her, huh, Neely? What, did she promise you a cushy lifestyle if you helped her keep it hush-hush? Is that the reason you've stayed here? Did you sell your soul to her? Or do you just stay for the life insurance money that she probably kicks back to you every month?" I screamed. Neely glared at me, looking mad as hell, but I was on a roll and I had absolutely no intentions of slowing down. "I saw his body, daddy's body hidden up in the attic, stuffed into some old trunk, as if he was some broken trinket that no one wanted, tossed away to be forgotten. How could y'all do that? How could you ruin my one chance of making something of myself, huh? You ruined it! I could have lived with my dad and actually had a normal childhood, but no, by killing him, momma condemned me to this shitty ass, mess of an upbringing that I've had! Look at me, Neely, look at this insane haircut she gave me. She is bat shit crazy!! How could you just stand aside and let her do whatever the hell she wanted. How could you let her kill my daddy?" I dropped to my knees, the intensity of the moment was too much. I began to sob.

Through my tears, I saw Neely's swollen ankles walk up beside me, as I felt the warmth of her hand touch my back. "Bliss, baby, come here honey," her voice, the one that had become so familiar to me was back. It is hard to explain how comforting her voice sounded to me. When I think back on it, it reminds me of sweet molasses, for some reason. It was just smooth and rich. I looked up at her, through raging tears, as she gently sat down beside me, and whispered in my ear. "My sweet, sweet, honey child; I did know about your father being in the attic and I am so sorry that I kept that from you. But, Bliss baby, there is somethin' ya need to know, and I want you to really hear me now. You listenin'?" I nodded as I sobbed loudly. She leaned in closer to my ear, and whispered, "Baby girl, yo' momma is many things, but she ain't no murderer. I ain't no murderer either, baby." I raised my head and looked into the eyes of my best friend, my only friend in the entire universe. The golden specks had returned, and I felt comfort. Neely took a deep ragged breath, as she continued, "Darlin' the hidin' of your daddy's body, that was all me. Yo' momma don't know nothin' about that. As far as Ms. Cecily Fontaine is concerned, yo' daddy is still alive and well. She thinks he ran off with some young bimbo, never to be seen again. I am the only person who knew what really happened to him. I was the one who put his body in that trunk in the attic, but I done it for yo' own good. Ya see, Miss Bliss, sweet baby girl, you're the one who took yo' daddy's life."

Chapter Six

I remember hearing the tick, tock, tick, tock of the grandfather clock that stood on the far wall of the study. Every tick sounded distant, and every tock echoed. There I sat, perfectly still, on the floor of the study. I could feel the warmth of Neely's arms wrapped around my body, in her desperate attempt to give me strength in my time of need. My eyes could not focus on anything, the entire room looked like a massive blur, which turned to spots, which faded into complete darkness.

A familiar smell woke me. It was a mix of frankincense oil, lavender oil, and rose oil. Neely's Feel Good Potion. She had used it on me on numerous occasions. She claimed that it was guaranteed to lift your spirits and make whatever was broken, whole again. Sometimes she would spray it throughout my room, sometimes she would put it in a cup of warm water, making it a tea for me to drink, but this particular time, she was sitting on the edge of the leather chaise lounge that I was laid out on, holding the potion bottle underneath my nose for me to smell. "Works every time," she boasted. Her face was hovering over mine so closely, that I could smell the sweet vanilla tobacco smell on her breath. I knew that she had probably smoked one of her pipes earlier that afternoon.

***

I adored the way Neely's pipes smelled. My mother did not approve of Neely smoking and she would not let her forget it. "Geez Louise, Neely, don't you know you're a woman? Pipes are for men. They are for men who don't care if they stink or not! Is that how you want to be regarded? As a manly woman who couldn't care less if she stinks up the whole block with her pipe tobacco smoke?" You could count on hearing a lecture at least once a week that went more or less like that. Neely would just smile her kind smile and say, "Now Ms. Cecily, I really don't think much about what other people's opinions are of me. Ya know I ain't never disrespected this house. I always take my pipes out in the yard." My mother, thinking she was going to have the last word, would say, "Well, Mr. Beauchamp was taking a jog last week and he saw you smoking away on the front walk. That does not bode well, Neely. He was discussing it with three other gentlemen that he was golfing with at the club, and they were laughing about it!" Neely would smile her infamous smile that I adored so much, it was the kind of smile that showed almost every single tooth in her mouth. She would reply to my mother, "well Ms. Cecily, you can tell Mr. Beauchamp and his golf buddies that I said, thank y'all for y'all's interest, but I am a nun." My mother would wrinkle her nose, slightly tilt her head to the side, and say. "You are not a nun, Neely, you are a maid. I know that, you know that, Mr. Beauchamp certainly knows that. I am sure that the other three gentlemen are well aware of your occupation as well. Anyone who is anyone in New Orleans knows that you are my maid, Neely. No one believes that you are a nun. So, if this is one of your silly jokes, I really don't have the time or the patience for it." Seeing how this irked my mother, just made Neely want to say the punchline of her joke even more. She would continue, with her alligator style smile on her face, "Ms. Cecily, you can tell Mr. Beauchamp and his little friends that I don't want none, I don't need none, and I certainly wouldn't ever be in such a desperate need of a man to give their gossiping asses none!" My mother would have a look of shock and horror on her face and briskly walk away. Yes, Neely had figured out how to shut my mother up, and I loved it!

***

I slowly sat up on the chaise lounge. "Here's a glass of cold water for ya, baby," Neely cooed, with that sweet molasses voice of hers. "Thank you," I whispered, as I took a slow drink. The cold water tasted so good and I could feel it surge through my body. It must have had a splash of the special water that Neely kept in an old bourbon bottle in her room. I asked her one time, when I was ten years old, what made the water special. She told me that a hoodoo priestess that she knew had blessed it and that it contained within it, the power to reconstruct your spirit and soul. I looked up at Neely and inquired, "Special hoodoo water?" "Mmhmm," she confirmed, "It heals all, baby."

Neely was a big boned woman, she probably weighed at least fifty pounds more than I did. Regardless of the weight difference, I was still surprised that she had managed to get me off of the study floor and onto the chaise lounge. It had to have been more than twenty steps away from the site of my reality check out. "How in the world did you get me all of the way over here?" I questioned. "Girl, you might think I'm an old lady, but this body still has some spitfire and gusto!" she mused, "and child please, ya know that ya weigh about as much as that skinny ass Calvin Klein girl that you stare at in yo' teenie-bopper magazines. What's her name…Kate or somethin' like that?" I laughed, thinking of the numerous occasions that Neely had walked into my room and caught me staring at the pretty supermodels that graced the pages of my magazines. I wasn't interested in them, like *interested* in them. I wasn't a lesbian or anything. I think my infatuation with them was caused by my longing to live a carefree life. I imagined that they had nothing in the world to worry about. I wanted that so badly.

The smile faded from my face as I allowed reality to sink in. The words Neely had uttered to me, seconds before my body got all protective of my mind and spirit, allowing me to faint in order to take the pain of the statement away, even if it was only for a little while. *I was the one who killed my father, me, when I was only a small child. How was that even possible? Why would I do such a hellacious thing? Was I an evil monster? Maybe I deserved the heinous treatment that I had been given. That must be the reason that my mother dislikes me. No, Neely said that momma didn't know about it. She said that the cognitive content that momma had was that daddy was basically a two timing son of a bitch, who had run off with another woman. How could momma not know that her husband had been killed by her own daughter?* My mind became a vortex of unanswered questions and half-baked opinions of myself. I knew I couldn't stall any longer. I needed to address the elephant in the room.

"How did I do it?" I asked. Neely drew a deep, ragged breath. I could sense that she had dreaded this inevitable moment for a very long time. "Bliss, sweet pea, I want ya to know that I kept all of this from ya for yo' own good. You know that I love ya, as if you's my own, and I would never ever want to do anything to upset ya or hurt ya, baby." she took another ragged breath, as if she was trying to summon the courage to continue. "Now, what I told ya was the God's honest truth. Yo' daddy never ran off, but Lord knows, every day that I worked in this house, I was wishin' that he would. Bliss baby, I know ya don't wanna hear this, but yo' daddy was one meanspirited, abusive man. He used to show his malevolent side to yo' momma almost every day, child. I hated seein' it, but I was told to mind my own damn business, so I did, I did for as long as I could, Miss Bliss." Tears were forming in Neely's eyes. She was a strong woman, and I knew that this was serious business if it made her emotional. My eyes stayed locked on hers as I supportively nodded my head, as if to coax her to continue. "For years he would drag his whiskey-soaked, drunk ass home from what he would claim was another late night at the office. Now you tell me, who the hell works until two o'clock in the morning at a damn office every night? I tell ya, Bliss, I didn't believe his sorry ass for one cotton-pickin' minute. I knew what he'd been doin'. Galavantin' around the French Quarter, lookin' for every call girl and bookie that he could find. Oh, ya momma knew it too. When she would question his whereabouts, he'd get madder than a wet hen. That's when his machismo crap would kick in. I swear, that man was horrible!" She paused for a moment, stifling a sob. Then she added, "I swore I wasn't going to intervene, I didn't want to get my ass fired. I hated being here when yo' daddy was actin' a fool, but I knew I had to stay to watch over ya. Yo' momma had fallen into a depression like I'd never seen, and I wasn't gonna to let ya slip by the wayside, or worse. Now honey, are ya sure that ya wanna hear about that fateful night, ya know, the one that made you take his life?" My skin felt hot. I knew that I had to find out, but part of me was afraid that I would hate myself if I knew the details.

I slowly nodded my head. "Okay then," she began, "you had witnessed Montgomery Fontaine's abuse for four years." "Montgomery," I interrupted her, "that was his name?" "Yep, Mr. Montgomery James Fontaine. Sounds like a regal name, don't it?" she asked. "Everyone used to call him, Monty for short. Sounds kind of cute, don't it?" I nodded once again and patted her thick thigh, as if to promise that I wouldn't interrupt her again, and that she could continue. "Anyways, you was only four years old, and you was the prettiest little thing. Ooh, child, I loved ya then, same as I love ya now. It just hurt me so bad when yo' daddy acted all crazy, waking ya up with his fits of rage. There you'd be all snug in yo' bed, dreamin' of being a princess, and you'd get woken up by him yellin' at yo' momma, poor thing. Well anyways, it was a scorchin' hot night in July of 1986. Yo' momma had gotten tired of yo' daddy's shit and she had run off, to Lord knows where. She had been gone for three weeks, with no word of her whereabouts. She just expected me to keep on keepin' on around here. I will never understand the inner workings of rich folk's minds, leaving her daughter with the maid, not giving a crap as to whether her four year old is doin' alright or not. Anywho, that ain't any of my concern. So in the wee hours of the mornin', we're talkin' three or four in the mornin', yo' daddy, Monty, had been out all night, paintin' the town red, the way he always did. I was rockin' ya back to sleep when he got home, in that same rockin' chair that sits in yo' room now, baby. You had a bad nightmare and I was comfortin' you. I had just gotten ya to drift back to sleep when that drunken asshole bursted into yo' bedroom, screamin' at ya, sayin' some crap like he wished that they had never had you. I usually kept to my own business and stayed out of his shit, but I was not going to let him mess with my baby girl. I told him to shut his damn mouth and leave ya alone, but he kept on rantin' and ravin' about how Ms. Cecily and him wouldn't have any problems if they didn't have you, all kinds of stupid shit like that. You were scared, child, oh honey, I felt so bad for you. You were clinging to me for dear life, hiding your face in my nightgown and screamin' at yo' daddy to leave us alone. I swear, Bliss, I thought he would take his drunk ass back downstairs and leave, but he was in rare form that night. He snatched you out of my arms and threw you into the wall. It knocked your poor little body clean out. I have never been so frightened in my life, I didn't know if you were still breathin' or not. Then Mr. Monty's belligerent ass made a bee line for your poor little body. He was hollerin' that he was gonna kill ya! Ya know I was not about to let that happen. I grabbed a big vase that was on yo' nightstand and I hit that man over the back of the head with all of my might. I hit the crap out of him. His drunk ass fell to the floor, I had knocked him out cold. Then I picked you up, baby and ran with ya to my room. I got out my Feel Good Potion and rubbed that oil all over your frail little body, then I had you breathe it in. It woke ya right up, I swear, it works every time. I told ya that it was going to be alright, I told ya that I would take care of ya. I grabbed my two pillows and took the pillow cases off. I told ya that we were going to get out of this place, away from yo' daddy. I began putting clothes and stuff in the pillow cases. I told ya to go grab some money from the old coffee can under the kitchen sink. I had saved up some money every week for years, for a rainy day, and honey that night had turned into a monsoon of trouble. I told ya that I would be right back, that I was going to get yo' favorite doll, Colette. Yep, you had Colette since ya was a baby and I knew ya couldn't sleep without her. It was a stupid move on my part. I should have just grabbed the money and left with ya, without looking back.

But I wasn't thinkin' straight, honey, I was frazzled and just tryin' to do the right thing."

Neely paused and I saw a big tear stream down her face and fall on my hand. I just sat, motionless. Hearing the events of that night was difficult and Neely's tear comforted me. I let it soak into my skin. *Her tears have healing powers*, I thought. I had always felt that Neely was magical. She exuded good vibes and an almost supernatural quality that calmed my spirit. Knowing how she took care of me, as a child, at the most vulnerable point in my life, made me love Neely more than I ever had. She was a mother to me. She had been the one to guide, guard, and direct me, and I would be forever thankful to her for that.

"Go ahead, Neely, I'm ready to hear the rest," I assured her. She wrapped her arms around me, laid my head on her shoulder, and continued in a hushed tone. "Bliss, baby, ya were always such a good girl, and ya still are. God, I can still hear yo' little feet running as fast as they could, pitter pattering towards the kitchen to grab that coffee can, as I made my way up the stairs to yo' room, to grab that doll for ya. When I made it to the top of the first flight of stairs, there was yo' daddy, head bleedin' and all, standin' in the hallway lookin' at me like he was Lucifer himself. I screamed bloody murder! He came boundin' down that hallway like a demon and grabbed me by the throat. I tried to run before he could get to me, but ya knows I ain't never been a physically fit woman. Ain't nobody gonna hire me to pose in the Sports Illustrated Swimsuit edition!" I couldn't help but giggle, even in the midst of the grievous recollection. I loved that Neely was so witty, I could only hope that I had gotten my personality from her.

"Well", she continued, with a sigh, "I think ya must have heard my scream resonate down the stairs and into the kitchen, where ya were fetching that coffee can of cash. The next minute or so, consisted of yo' daddy trying to kill my ass, and me desperately trying to live for you. He had me pinned down on the hardwood floor at the top of the stairs. He had his fingers around my neck and all of his weight sitting on my chest. I pushed and kicked with all of my might, but I could not get his crazy ass off of me. I think he must have also been on cocaine, or Lord knows what, that night. I'm tellin' ya, it couldn't have just been the whiskey. It was like that man had super human strength that night. You are the reason that I fought so hard, baby girl. I knew that if he was victorious, Mr. Montgomery Fontaine would have surely killed ya, and I wasn't about to let that happen, no way, no how! So, there I am, trying to pry his fingers off of my neck, desperately gasping for air, knowing damn well that my dark brown skin was surely turning cerulean by that point. I was struggling to keep consciousness. In the midst of all of that, I heard the pitter patter of yo' little feet, baby girl, I heard ya scream so loudly, then all at once the pressure of that evil man's fingers went completely limp. I choked and coughed, gasping for the sweet oxygen that my body so craved. Once I had my breath, I saw it. I saw yo' daddy lying face down on the floor, blood covering the back of his white dress shirt. I saw the blood-stained cleaver wedged into the back of the head of that man's lifeless body, and I saw you, Bliss. You were standing there, a beautiful angel, my saving grace, in your pink satin nightgown, without a tear in your eye."

Chapter Seven

I seriously deserve to win an Academy Award, I thought, as I was seated in the dining room, across from my mother. Although I now was aware that she was not a fiendish murderer, she still made my skin crawl, and I had to sit politely, acting as if everything was wonderful. My jaw tightened, and I clenched my teeth together as hard as I could. It took every bit of self control that I could muster, not to shout out the many questions that I had swirling through my head. I wanted to look right at her stiff, overly botoxed face, and scream! *What kind of person runs off for weeks at a time, abandoning their four year old child? What kind of a mother would stay in an abusive household, allowing their child to be in harm's way?* Neely had said that my mother was under my daddy's spell, "and when you's under a love spell like that, with a man that good lookin', sometimes you just can't tell wrong from right, sugar." I didn't like that Neely was giving my momma excuses for being an unfit mother, like I should be okay with the fact that she'd been punishing me in diabolical ways for years. In my opinion, it would take a very weak-minded woman to stay with a man like Montgomery Fontaine, I didn't care how handsome and rich he was. The fact of the matter was that she should not have forced me into that distorted version of a childhood. She should have chosen her child's well-being over a man that treated her like dog shit. I knew that deep down, Neely agreed with me. Neely was a woman of gumption. She would never allow herself to fall under the spell of a barbaric man, like Monty. I knew, for damn sure, that if my mother had loved me even half as much as Neely did, that she would have had the guts to take me away from harm, away from Montgomery Fontaine. If she had done that, the terrifying night would never have happened. If she had done that, we could have lived normal, happy lives. If she had done that, she wouldn't have turned into a hateful person. But no, she had been too chicken shit to leave. She sealed her fate, and in turn, mine, when she chose him over her own daughter.

There she sat, eight feet away, across from me at the dining room table. Everything about her aggravated me. I could hear her chewing her bite of lamb chop. I could hear her swallow a mouthful of Chardonnay. I squirmed in my seat. "What is the matter with you?" she asked in a disapproving tone. "Nothing," I said through gritted teeth. "Then you need to eat your dinner, young lady. Don't you realize that there are starving children around the world? You really need to think of others, Bliss, and stop being so selfish and entitled," she scolded. I wanted to jump out of my skin! Of all people on this earth to call me entitled. Talk about the pot calling the kettle black! I looked up from my plate, and glared right at her. *I don't know who you think you are to call me entitled, Cecily Fontaine,* I wanted to say, but instead I just sat there, staring bullets at her perfectly lined eyes. "Bliss, really," she continued, "are you mad about your hair? You cannot be angry with me about the haircut. That is just your vanity. You brought that haircut upon yourself. Now what kind of a mother would I be if I had just let you get a big head about winning those pageants? I could see that you were becoming vain and I had no choice but to punish you. The Lord does not want us to be conceited and vain, Bliss. Being vain is sinful, you know. You should thank your lucky stars that you have a mother that noticed the signs, and found a way to cut you down to size and make you realize that you have absolutely nothing to be conceited about. I'm just glad I nipped it in the bud, before it was too late." I felt my ears get hot, I looked down at my plate. The lamb chop, mashed potatoes, and wedge salad that Neely had so carefully prepared, looked like a swirl of colors, at that moment. I was infuriated by my mother's comments, so infuriated, that I could not see straight. My brain was flooded with a plethora of insults that I could shoot back at momma, but I had endured enough drama, reliving the past with Neely that afternoon.

My mother had decided to spend her entire afternoon at Magnolia Country Club, following that morning's brunch with her clique, which gave Neely ample time to fill me in on details, pertaining to the night that I took my father's life. Neely said that not a soul knew about my father's death, except for her, myself, and one other person. A person that she trusted, "to the moon and back," as she put it. She told me that it was someone that had been an intricate part of each one of the many lives that she had lived. The person was a woman named Dahlia, who lived in a small, but magical, house on the outskirts of the French Quarter.

***

Neely told me that the moment she realized that I had taken Montgomery Fontaine's life, she scooped me up and took me to my bedroom. She said that she did not want the reality of the moment to frighten me, therefore she made a game of packing a suitcase of my things. "Let's see how many pair of panties you can grab out of yo' dresser drawer and put into the suitcase on yo' bed, by the time I count to ten," she instructed. Neely did the same thing with socks, dresses, and shoes. Before she knew it, my suitcase was all packed, my doll, Colette, was tucked under my arm, and we were getting into the car that my parents had purchased for Neely to run her errands in. I had ridden in the car with Neely many times, on trips to the dry cleaner and the grocery store, but I had never ridden in the car with her in the middle of the night. Neely said that I looked frightened during the ride, and that she kept telling me that everything was gonna be alright. She said that she actually taught me how to do the calming breath that night, but that the memory of it had been "taken right out of my pretty little head," along with the rest of my memories of that night. She must have taught me her famous breathing technique a couple of years later, hence my recollection of it at six years old. Neely shared with me that it took "way too damn long" for Dahlia to get to the door that night. She said that we probably knocked on it about twenty times before Dahlia emerged in her long, tribal print robe, and head wrap. "That woman is the most spiritually-connected person that I have ever known, she could predict a rainstorm two years ahead of time, if she wanted to. She knew we was comin' that night, Bliss. She was just enjoyin' her beauty sleep a little too much, to answer the door in any kind of hurry." she confided with a smile.

Neely claimed that she didn't have to speak a word to Miss Dahlia about what had happened at our house. Dahlia already knew. She could sense it the moment that she saw us. "Come on in here, sweet child, everything is going to be just fine, you'll see." Dahlia assured, as she nodded at Neely and told her that she would make things right with me, and that Neely could come back in three days' time to pick me up.

Apparently, Neely left, and headed back to the scene of the crime. She explained that, once she returned to the house, she grabbed an old comforter from the trunk of her car. She added that she had kept the comforter in the trunk because she had intended on giving it to one of her friends from the church that she sometimes attended. "I swear, Miss Bliss, that lady had five kids, no husband, and no money. I always felt so bad for her, so I thought that next time I was at church I would give the comforter to her, along with some of the clothes you'd outgrown, and maybe some of our leftovers from the week. Ya know, just to help her out a bit." *That's the reason his body was covered with that old dingy thing,* I thought.

She said she drug my daddy's body up to the third floor, into the attic, knowing that my mother would never step foot into such a filthy place. "Then I rolled him into an empty trunk that was stashed away up there. I knew in my head that yo' momma wasn't gonna ever go in there, but just in case, I covered his body with the comforter, makin' it look like that was all that was stored in that trunk." Neely continued, "then, I made sure I cleaned the hell out of the hallway and the staircase, making sure that there were absolutely no traces of blood. As far as the cleaver goes, I just left that thing wedged into his skull. Ya must not have seen it when ya looked in the trunk, baby, because I probably laid his body face up. The back of his head looked disgusting and I couldn't bear to look at it." I understood that, as I remembered throwing up when I had discovered the body, two years prior. It was close to seven o'clock in the morning, by the time that she had finished ridding our house of all of the evidence, but she wasn't quite done yet.

She grabbed a piece of my father's business letterhead, from his office in the house, and proceeded to write a letter to his business partner. Neely had practiced copying my father's handwriting, for years. She had been the one who was told, on numerous occasions, to write checks for the gardener, the handyman, the pool cleaner, and the interior decorator. Neely was an intelligent woman, making it easy for her to draft the fake letter. "I wrote that letter so good, Bliss. I acted like I was yo' daddy writin' it. There was no way, yo' daddy's business partner, Mr. Jacob Devereaux, was going to be suspicious at all. Hell, he knew all of the runnin' around yo' daddy was doin'. He hated it. Mr. Devereaux was an upstanding, serious business man. I knew that he would be happy to bid adieu to yo' father. The letter read somethin' like this:

Jacob,

I have met the woman of my dreams and we were going to run away together to get away from my wife, Cecily. I regret that I will be leaving all of the weight of the business on you. I greatly appreciate all of the effort that you have put into building the company into what it is today, but as you know, the heart wants what the heart wants. I would not be able to live with myself, if I were to ignore my feelings for Adelaide. I hate that I will be leaving Cecily and my daughter, Bliss with such a heavy burden. I want only the best for them, therefore, with much thought and consideration, I have decided that I would like to cash out on my share of the company. I would like for that amount to be given to Cecily and Bliss, instead of myself. I want them to be able to maintain the lifestyle that they have grown accustomed to, the lifestyle that they deserve. I will have no problem making a life for me and my soon-to-be new bride, Adelaide. I already have a few things in the works, so there is no need to worry about me. I do not want any bad jus-jus on my soul. This is goodbye, as I will be leaving today.

I am proud of everything that you and I have accomplished together, but I am looking forward to beginning a new chapter in my life.

Best Regards,

Monty

"I made it sound all professional, Bliss, there was no way it wasn't gonna work," she told me. After she drafted the letter, she faxed it to Mr. Jacob Devereaux from my father's home fax machine. "Then I went and took myself a warm shower and got dressed into clean clothes. I made sure I shredded the blood-stained nightgown that I was wearin'. I shredded that thing to pieces, so that there was no way anyone would find it, then I went out the back door and walked all the way to the very back edge of our property line, ya know, underneath that magnolia tree, and I buried the shredded pieces of that nightgown."

Neely said that I stayed at Miss Dahlia's house for three days, as Dahlia did her magic on me, cleansing my mind and spirit from the memories of that night. "That was the hard part for me, child, the waitin'. Lord, I hated havin' to wait those three days. I wanted to see ya, I needed to hold ya, but I'll tell ya, Dahlia knows what she's doin', and when she says three days, she means it. She had told me it had to be three full days for the magic to stick and your memory of that night to be gone for good." Neely continued, "Ooh sugar, I was a nervous wreck, not knowin' if yo' momma was gonna show up at the house within those three days you was with Dahlia. I didn't know what the hell I was gonna tell her, 'bout where ya was, but I just took my chances."

Neely told me that the doorbell rang on the second day, and that it had scared the living daylights out of her. She said that she half expected that it was going to be the police, questioning the whereabouts of my father. "It was the mail carrier with some certified mail for Mrs. Cecily Fontaine. I signed for it, and looked at the return address. It was the address of yo'daddy's office building. I knew that it must be the check for yo' daddy's share of the company. Praise Jesus! We was gonna be just fine."

Neely said that by the time the third day rolled around, my momma was still M.I.A. Neely spent that entire evening pacing back and forth throughout the house. She had to wait until exactly four thirty eight in the morning to pick me up, because when Dahlia says, "exactly three days", you don't question it. Neely showed up on Dahlia's doorstep at 4:38am, on the dot. I was smiling and as happy as I could be. I gave Dahlia a big hug and told her thank you for having me visit, then I squeezed Neely so hard that she said she felt like she was hugging a professional wrestler. Neely said that Dahlia gave her a potion for me to drink once we got home, which would seal the spell and make me forget that I had ever visited her house.

From what Neely told me, I drank the potion down, with no complaints, once we arrived safely home. She tucked me into bed, as it was around five o'clock in the morning, and told me to get a few more hours of sleep. Then Neely, my guardian angel, sat herself down in the rocking chair in the corner of my bedroom, watching her once again, innocent baby girl fall fast asleep.

***

Chapter Eight

The spring of 2000 feels like somewhat of a blur to me. Once Neely had confided in me, on that April evening, my mind could think of nothing else. I wasn't consumed by the gruesomeness of everything that had happened on the fateful night, thirteen years prior. I didn't focus on the negative, that's just the way I've always been, *optimistic, with a capital 'O'*, as Neely would often say. "I always knew you was gonna be a good spirited, happy girl," she'd tell me on numerous occasions, "I knew, before you was even born that you was gonna be somethin' special; a wild-eyed dreamer, starry-eyed as they come; a quixotic girl." Neely would not let me forget how special that she thought I was. It was no secret that Neely had been the one to name me when I was born. She had been my parent's maid since they moved into the antebellum mansion in 1978. She said that the house was dreadfully boring for the first four years that she worked there, until I made my debut on a "hotter than hell" evening in June.

$$***$$

My father had, unapologetically, missed my introduction into the world, as he was in Los Angeles on a business trip. My parents had not planned on having children. My mother did not possess one single maternal bone in her body, and was insanely self-centered. My father was obviously an unabashed playboy with anger issues. Thank God I had Neely. She spared me the details, but I easily pieced together the neurosis of the whole situation. My mother got pregnant with me in a desperate attempt to put a stop to my dad's shenanigans. She probably thought that having a baby would settle him down. My mother had assumed that Montgomery Fontaine would magically morph into an upstanding man once he became a father. A man who wasn't a sloppy drunk, a man who didn't run around town looking for any call girl that he could find, and most importantly of all, she'd hoped that, by becoming a father, the physical abuse would stop.

Neely had been the first person to hold me. When the people at the hospital asked my momma what she wanted to name me, she had said that she didn't know and that names didn't matter that much. She told them that they could just write down any name that they wanted to. "Names do matter, baby," Neely had told me when I was a child, every time that I brought up the day of my birth. "I named you Bliss because the moment I first looked at ya, I knew that's what ya were filled to the brim with, happiness and bliss. Child, most babies take a long while to start smilin', not you, no ma'am. I swear, ya smiled right at me the first moment I laid my eyes on ya. A baby destined fo' greatness, I knew it then, and I know it now. But ya know, when I suggested the name, Bliss, Miss Cecily looked right at me like I'd lost my damned mind," Neely would tell me, wearing that alligator smile of hers that I loved so much. Then she would continue on with her story, "yo' momma, always havin' to ruin the moment, said somethin' like that Bliss wasn't a real name, and somethin' else about me not carin' what people would think. Then I told her that you was the most exquisite and the most euphoric baby that this world had ever seen. I told her that I could feel it in my bones that Bliss was the name for ya, that you was deservin' of an extraordinary name. I told her that Bliss was the only name pretty enough to do ya any justice."

***

My mother wasn't shy about telling her friends the story about the day I was born. I often overheard her talking to her coterie of surgically altered friends, while they were brunching at our house, which was a frequent occurrence, due to Neely's amazing kitchen skills. The topic was usually brought up while my mother introduced me to any of the newbies in the group. You could bet on at least one of them complementing my mother for choosing such a beautiful and unique name for me. My mother would hyperbolize every bit of the story, leaving out anything that could possibly make her look bad, which, except for the whole, her pushing me out of her body thing, was pretty much all of it. She always took credit for choosing my name, always. I didn't understand how someone could be so phony. I was, of course, expected to repress my annoyance. Cecily Fontaine had an image to uphold and she expected me to politely smile and keep my mouth shut. *If only these women knew what I really thought about my mother, it would shock the hell out of them.* I would think, as I stood nodding and smiling, in the designer dress and pumps that my mother had purchased for me to wear. It was always a plain colored dress and solid color, old lady looking pumps, every damn time. She didn't like for me to stand out too much, in her mind, different was a bad word. I knew that another reason that she wanted me to look basic was because she was not going to let me outshine her.

Cecily Fontaine had relied on her looks for her entire life. Nothing else mattered to her, not even her own daughter. I had never pitied my mother, but something about that, made me feel bad for her. *She doesn't understand life, the meaning of our existence,* I thought. I knew that I was an old soul. I could just feel it. It also helped that Neely agreed with me. She told me all of the time that I was an old soul, wise beyond my years, and that I had probably lived more than a hundred lives already. "That's the only way you can learn things, Bliss, by livin'," Neely would say, "the whole point of life is for the universe to teach us lessons that our souls can carry on with us into our next lifetime. Most of us don't remember anything 'bout our past lives, or so we think. But, I'm tellin' ya, Bliss, our higher selves remember, and that's why our conscious helps to guide us through life, using what we've learned. There ain't no coincidences, honey, everything happens for a reason. People and situations are put into our journey to either teach us somethin', or to help us along the way. That's what you and me is, we's kindred spirits, baby." I believed that, with all of my heart. Neely was in my life to be a guide for me, to soften the blow of the insults shot at me by my mother.

 I usually did a commendable job of suppressing my thoughts and blending in at the brunches hosted by my mother at our house. I would listen as they talked about who the best plastic surgeon was, only allowing my mind to wander about fifty times. I would imagine how I could disappear from the miserable moment that I was constrained into sitting through. Spontaneous combustion seemed to be the front runner, most of the time. *Geez, these women fake laugh, like it's going out of style,* I thought. Listening to them gossip and giggle, whilst they devoured Neely's Cajun crabcake bites. They were delicious little bits of heaven topped with remoulade. I swear, I don't think there was a chef in all of New Orleans that could top Neely's cooking. Of course, upon receiving compliments on the food, my mother would never mention that Neely had prepared the food. She would flat out lie, telling those uppity snobs that she had gotten the food catered from whichever fancy-schmancy French Quarter restaurant was the most highly coveted at that particular moment. *How rude,* I would think, *Neely worked damn hard in that kitchen with no thanks whatsoever!*

***

It was a Tuesday, in late May, when I found that my self-control had its limits. It was the first brunch, since the 'Edward Scissorhands on crack' haircut punishment, that was to be held at our house. My mother had not been the host of their weekly brunches since sometime in January. I stood at the top of the stairs on the second floor, looking down at the foyer. My hands were clammy. I took a deep calming breath, just like Neely had taught me, as I prepared myself for the act of defiance that I was about to embark upon. I felt as if I had lived within an intricate pattern of dominoes and that, with this act of defiance, I was going to push over the first domino, which in turn, would cause the entire structure of subjugation that my mother had built for the past seventeen and a half years, to demolish.

Earlier that morning, while I was in the shower; attempting to wash every bit of pride off of my body and out of my insane excuse for hair; preparing myself to put on the dress, the shoes, and the fake smile; my mother went into my bedroom and laid out what was to be my ensemble for the brunch. I emerged from the bathroom, wearing my terry cloth robe, my confidant that had witnessed the demise of my beauty, the evening of the awful haircut. It lended its comfort as I walked down the hallway towards my bedroom. My stomach began to feel weak as I felt dread pour over my body. Something was about to happen, I could feel it.

Neely had told me for years, that I had a strong third eye and that I was a natural empath. I could sense when things were about to happen. Sometimes my mind gave me clues as to what to expect and sometimes I would just have a feeling surge over me. "We just have to decalcify that pineal gland of yours, then ya will be able to see more and feel more. Just as you was intended to," Neely would tell me. I had not yet delved into what all of that actually meant, but there was no denying that the feeling that had consumed my body and spirit that late May morning, was not a positive one. I continued down the hallway, towards my bedroom door, inhaling deeply in an attempt to shake the feeling that had come over me.

Upon entering my sacred space, I saw it, and immediately understood the reason that dread had consumed me, just moments before. Laid out on my floral comforter, was not only the typical dress and pumps that my mother expected me to wear to the brunch, which was scheduled to begin in twenty five minutes. Next to the dress, my mother had laid out a long, blonde wig. *You have got to be kidding me,* I thought. *Well played, Cecily Fontaine, I must give you kudos, as you played a card that I was not expecting. Wow, you have some nerve! Psychotically chopping away at my hair, making me look insane; then, keeping me in the house for the next five weeks, in an attempt to hide me, like I'm the Hunchback of Notre Dame, or something. I didn't expect to go to the brunch, Mother. I expected to be able to hide out in my room, wrapped up in a good book, knowing damn well that you didn't want the embarrassment of me showing my crazy ass looking haircut to any of your comrades. But no, you told me last night at the dinner table that you wanted for me to be at the brunch, that you wouldn't allow me to stay upstairs. You told me that it would make you look rude and ill-mannered in front of your friends to allow your teenage daughter to hide out in her room. Now I know why you were so insistent about me coming to the brunch. You had planned to have me wear this fake ass looking wig, in order to allow yourself to still look like the mom of the year.*

I knew that Neely would be busy preparing the food in the kitchen, therefore going to her to vent about my disdain for momma was out of the question, at least for the time being. *There is no way in hell that I am going to wear that thing, I thought. She is only worried about how it will make her look. She doesn't give a damn about my sensitivity.* At that point, I was down to twenty minutes of primping time, so I got to it. I quickly applied my makeup, combed and blow-dried what was left of my hair, and got dressed into the ensemble that my mother had laid out for me. I had on the typical designer dress and grandma looking pumps, but I left the wig lying on my bed.

My footsteps echoed on the hardwood floor of the hallway, as I approached the staircase that would lead me downstairs to the unveiling of my rebelliousness. My head tingled, in the familiar way that it had, two years before, when I had ventured into the unknown of the attic. I had a major breakthrough that day, two years ago. My third eye was telling me that, by me walking into the dining room and debuting my new look, so graciously given to me by Cecily herself, I would have not only a breakthrough, but a turning point in my life. The imaginary ants that were crawling all over not only my head, but my entire body, by this point, must have known it too. Last time, they had warned me not to go into the attic, in their tiny voices. Not this time. They knew better. I was on a mission to unveil the injustices of the Fontaine house, and no one was going to detour me. I whispered a mantra to myself, with each step that I took, "you were born for a time such as this, you were born for a time such as this," I said over and over to myself. It seemed like the hallway was never going to end. *Dang, hallway, have you been eating your vegetables or something? 'Cause it sure feels like you've grown*, I thought, as I took the last few strides necessary to reach the top of the stairs, also known as, the point of no return.

Chapter Nine

I made my descent down the stairs swiftly. My spirit was abuzz. I was a girl with something to say and I was not going to be silenced. *The gag is off and the jig is up,* I thought, as I rounded the corner into the formal dining room. To say that I made quite an entrance that day, is an understatement. I think every single one of those bleach blonde, extension-wearing, overly teased, helmet heads turned and looked at me in shock and awe as I strutted into the room. It took all of a nano second for me to know where the queen bee herself was. I could feel the negativity exuding from every inch of her body. I looked right into her piercing green eyes. *I am your victim no more, Cecily Fontaine,* I chanted in my mind, hoping that her demented noesis would take note. It felt like we were having a showdown at the O.K. Corral, except instead of a gun, I was wielding my intent and my firmness of purpose as my weapons of choice. That woman marched up to me, faster than a hot knife through butter. "Bliss Marie, I suggest you get your butt up to your bedroom this instant, young lady," she whispered through gritted teeth. I smiled, looked right at her, in all of her black aura glory, and as loud and proud as I could, I responded, "Momma, I find it rather amusing that you think that I'm going to actually obey your crazy ass! I was told I had to attend this brunch, so here I am, attending this brunch. I am here, just like you wanted. Just because you wanted to hide this screwball lookin' haircut that you gave me, doesn't mean that I have to oblige. Making me attend this brunch is the last order that you are ever going to give me, I can promise you that. "Then I turned my attention to my mother's guests, "Now, if all y'all could stop starin' at me, and continue to enjoy yourselves, that would be just peachy. I don't know about y'all, but I am ready to eat the best food in all of Louisiana, which, by the way, has been prepared by my mother's maid, and my best friend, Neely Johnson."

I proceeded to make my way through the sea of my mother's high cotton friends, as I made a beeline for the hors d'oeuvres table. I had a mouthful of Neely's Cajun crabcake bite, remoulade running down the side of my mouth and everything, as I made my way to the kitchen to tell Neely all about how I had told my momma off in front of everyone. "Ooh child, Miss Cecily is gon' be fit to be tied when this party is over! You better watch yo' back girl, ya know how ya momma is, sneakier than the devil himself. She is gonna have one hell of a hissy fit. You might wanna sleep in my room tonight, baby," Neely suggested. The reality of the aftermath of my outburst of independence began to sink in and my stomach began to feel as if it was auditioning to be the featured acrobat in Cirque du Soleil. I felt shaky, *what will she do to get back at me?* I wondered. It was inevitable that she was going to formulate some sort of evil revenge. *Lord, have mercy, I hope she doesn't have any damn voodoo dolls of me! Shit, now I'm the deer and she's the hunter. It's her move, and I just have to wait for it.*

I was in the middle of thinking of all of the horrible acts of wrath that my mother could cast upon me, when she bursted into the kitchen. "There you are," she stormed, "I just wanted to let your sassy ass know that you've now officially bought yourself a new home. Don't you worry your pretty little head about it, you'll probably like it, you can have all of the fits you want to in there, and no one will give a damn. There will be exactly no damns given. Do you understand me? None! You can be as wild-eyed and impulsive as you want to in there. I assure you, it will just add to your experience," she said as she patted my head and snickered, before turning to walk menacingly out into the dining room. *Why the hell does she keep saying 'in' there?* I wondered. I looked at Neely, who stared at me with fear in her eyes. "What did she mean by that?" I asked. Before Neely could answer, I heard my mother's voice cut through the swinging door that led from the kitchen, into the dining room. "You will have to excuse my daughter, ladies," she started, "Bliss is a troubled young lady," she continued, as she pretended to stifle a very 'woe is me', Scarlett O'Hara style sob. I walked towards the swinging door and leaned in as closely as I could, being extremely careful not to press against the door, as I wanted my identity as an eavesdropper to go undetected. "You poor thing, we had no idea what you've been dealing with all of these years." One of momma's sheep said. Then, using her most dramatic 'feel sorry for me, please, I'm begging you' voices, my mother continued, "yes, my daughter has been fighting her mental illness for years, it has been her demon. I have prayed and prayed, ever since she was just a little thing, that the Lord would give me strength to make it through each day. Y'all just cannot imagine what kind of courage it takes to take care of someone as mentally disturbed as my daughter, Bliss, bless her heart. I mean what y'all just witnessed was absolutely nothin' compared to the aggressive outbursts that she has on a daily basis. Poor child, she must have gotten that from her daddy, because no one on my side of the family is crazy. She has gotten so abusive and violent towards me, y'all wouldn't believe the things she's done. I mean, y'all saw the way her hair looks, yeah she did that to herself, poor thing, during one of her fits. I just praise Jesus that I was at home when it happened, and that I was smart enough to talk her down from stabbing herself with the shears, then she turned them on me and I thought she was going to take my life. I just kept sayin' the Lord's Prayer and it got me through it. Bliss finally snapped out of it, but she is a firecracker, I never know when she's gonna go off. That girl can't control herself, she has issues! "

It took every bit of restraint in my body, not to explode through that swinging door and tear that woman to pieces with my words. Lord knows, I could have eaten her alive with my wit, but Cecily Fontaine knew exactly what she was doing. She knew that playing this hand meant that I wouldn't come barreling through the door, raising cane, for fear of making myself look crazy, and in turn proving her right to all of her blonde robots that were listening. I peeked through the crack between the door frame and the actual door. I could see all of the women in their Ann Taylor suits, holding their mimosas, and nodding their heads, sympathetically to my mother. "I swear, Cecily Fontaine could start a damn cult if she wanted to," I whispered to Neely, "she's got every upper crust female in New Orleans in there, just feelin' sorry for her. Believing every damn word that she says." Neely didn't respond, so I turned around to look at her, but she had vanished. *Where the hell did she go? Maybe nature was calling,* I thought, as I turned my ear back to the door in order to hear more. I heard my momma continue, "I wasn't going to tell y'all, because, as y'all know, I am not the type that likes for people to feel sorry for me." *Yeah right,* I thought, *and I'm Justin Timberlake!* She went on, "it saddens me, it really does. I mean it just breaks my heart, but I know it's what's best for Bliss, and that's all that really matters. I have, with great agony and despair, come to the realization that Bliss does not belong in this home with me." Amen to that, I thought, great, maybe this is her way of saying that she will allow me to go off to college, I could finally get away from her!

Against my mother's wishes and behind her back, I had applied to three universities. It was risky, as I knew she would not want me to attend college, as she had always had Neely homeschool me, in an attempt to keep me away from outside influences and ideals. I actually got accepted into all three universities; New York University, The University of Texas, and Louisiana State University. Neely was the one who always checked the mail, and she was the one who actually encouraged me to apply, so I knew that my secret was safe. Of course, Neely was ecstatic when I got the news of my acceptance to each school. She even did her little happy dance. It was hilarious! She would swivel her wide hips in a circular motion, as if she was hula hooping or something, while her arms were doing a slightly altered version of 'raise the roof'.

My attention was quickly propelled back to my mother's announcement. *Which college is she going to let me attend?* I pondered as my mother, stifling another fake sob, continued,

"Tomorrow will be a very difficult day for our family, as I will be checking Bliss into the Orleans Parish Psychiatric Hospital."

Chapter Ten

I felt as if the wind had been knocked out of me. I had not seen that coming. It was an extreme measure, even for Cecily Fontaine. The hot tears that I had grown accustomed to showing up in my eyes, made their entrance once again. I fanned my face with my hands as I gasped for breath. I didn't have time to move, when the swinging door flew open, hitting me smack dab in the face, as my mother stormed into the kitchen. "Did you enjoy my speech?" She asked, as she narrowed her eyes and grinned at me, as if she couldn't have been more pleased with herself. "Momma, you've truly gone off your rocker this time," I growled, "I guess I need to start calling you Joan Crawford. Nice little show you put on out there, but I know you can't be serious." "Oh, Bliss, I am completely serious," she confessed, "All it will take is for me to make a call to the psychiatric hospital, telling them every disturbed thing I can conjure up about you. Don't worry sweet 'ums, you'll be a shoe in for sure," she said, while condescendingly patting my head. "I will tell them what a liar you arc, I will tell them that you are the insane one!" I yelled.

The hot tears, that I had tried so hard to blink back, began pouring down my face. They weren't tears of weakness, they were brought upon by my hatred for my mother. I knew that she would assume that my crying was a sign of me being submissive to her, and I couldn't stand that. I needed for her to realize that I was strong, that I had a voice, and that I would not let her dictate my life any longer. I turned around, my crying eyes, full of not only hot tears, but full of fury as well, as I screamed, "I will not be imprisoned! I have a purpose. I am smart, I am a beautiful soul. I am meant to do fabulous, wonderful, meaningful things in this life. I am sorry that you have never been able to see that. How sad for you. You have missed out on having amazing experiences with a daughter that would have been the most loving, caring daughter in the world to you, had you given her the chance. I will no longer sit back and let you strip my happiness away from me. I am in control of myself and my destiny, you are not! You have absolutely no power or control over me, Cecily Fontaine. I choose to live a fulfilled life. I will not sit back and watch the world pass me by. I will live a life that matters!"

She just stood there, staring at me. The smell of orange juice and champagne lingered. Judging by the rant she was on, I knew that she had probably already downed at least five mimosas. She showed no emotion, no reaction to the invisible gauntlet that I had just thrown down, right there in the middle of the kitchen floor. She just stared at me with blank, hollow eyes. I don't even think that she blinked for a good two minutes. Had momma finally checked out of reality and gone to her happy place? That usually didn't happen with mimosas, it usually took tequila to take Cecily Fontaine into La-La Land.

I stood and stared right back at her, glaring intensely. She looked like a little girl, just staring blankly, as if she was naïve and confused. My mind echoed over and over again; *do not play into her ploy. Don't feel sorry for her, she wants to reel you in. She wants to make you back down, so that she can shoot you right through the heart as soon as you are within her grasp. Stay strong, Bliss, you are a girl of gumption, you are a free thinker. You had every right to yell at her like that.* We were both silent, having a third grade style staring contest. The only noise was the hum of the refrigerator, and the muffled voices of the brunch attendees gossiping, probably comparing me to Jack Torrance from The Shining.

Our staring contest ended when we heard loud footsteps coming down the short hallway that connected the butler's pantry to the kitchen. Thud, shuffle, thud, shuffle. I knew those sounds, it was Neely. "Bliss, baby, where ya at?" Neely's voice echoed. She sounded out of breath and in a hurry. Before I could answer her, she rounded the corner to see my mother and I standing between the walk-in pantry and the granite countertop island, that stood in the middle of our kitchen. "Why are you so concerned as to Bliss' whereabouts, Neely?" my mother inquired. Then she turned her attention to me, "Bliss, you can just go up to your room and try to enjoy your last day in this house," she said, sarcastically. "We will be leaving in the morning to take you to your new permanent residence at seven o'clock sharp, so make sure that you are ready." She said, with a deviant smile on her face. She kept her eyes steady on me, as she continued, "Neely the guests are not going to serve themselves. I would appreciate it if you would make yourself useful and do your job." "Yes ma'am," Neely replied, as she watched Cecily Fontaine vanish through the swinging door, into the dining room.

Neely shuffled over to me quickly and embraced me, with one of the best hugs that she had ever given to me. Then she leaned back and touched my face. "Are you okay, baby girl?" she asked. My tears began to pour again. I didn't wipe them, neither did Neely. She just looked at me with her kind eyes, the golden specks dancing in a sea of chocolate. "It's alright, honey, them are healin' tears. You just let 'em on out, ya hear?" The tears represented my fear and anxiety of what was to come in the morning. They poured down my cheeks, under my chin, and down my neck. "Did you hear what she said, Neely?" I asked. "About the loony bin?" I continued, "I am not going to waste away in some cell with padded walls! I'm so damn claustrophobic, I wouldn't last one day!" "Hush now, child," Neely comforted, "I'll take care of you. Ain't nobody gonna be able to take my baby and lock her away, no ma'am."

Neely began to gently lead me down the hallway that she had emerged from just minutes before. "I really needed you, Neely, when Momma was actin' all cuckoo. Bad timing for you to run off to the powder room," I told her. Neely stayed silent. *Geez, she's waddling super fast,* I thought. "What's the damn rush, Neely?" I asked. "Are you impersonating Jackie Joyner-Kersee, or somethin'," I teased, with a slight smile. Neely's face stayed as serious as can be, no sign of a smirk. She usually enjoyed my witty comments. *What the hell is up with her?* I wondered.

Once we passed the butler's pantry, I started to turn left to go up the back staircase to my room. *I don't care that I am almost eighteen years old*, I thought, *I just want to lay on my bed and hold Colette.* I swear, that doll had soaked up enough of my tears over the years to fill a whole alligator infested swamp. I felt Neely place her hand on my left shoulder as she gently nudged me away from the staircase, bringing us further down the back hallway, towards her room. *She probably wants to make sure that I'm not going to go to any extreme measures, I thought, today being my last day in the real world and all. No, Neely knows that I would never do anything like that, doesn't she? Maybe she just wants to give me some of her magic hoodoo water to calm my nerves. I just wish she would let me go to the comfort of my room and cry.*

I started to veer left once again, when we reached the doorway to Neely's room. She placed her hand on my left shoulder again, and gingerly pushed me further down the hallway, as she looked over her shoulder, down the hallway behind us. We were heading toward the door at the end of the hallway. That door led to the garage. "Neely, will you please tell me what the plan is here?" I exclaimed, as she opened the door, leading me through it. The overhead garage door was already open. "Neely!" my mother's condescending voice echoed down the hallway. We turned around and saw her standing at the far end of the hallway, looking furious as hell.

Neely looked right into my eyes, as she shuffled me quickly towards the car that was parked in the garage, the engine was already running. It was the car that Neely had for nearly twenty two years now. Her errand car. The same car that she had used to take me to Miss Dahlia's house the night that I took my daddy's life. I could hear my mother's designer heels clicking faster on the hardwood floor of the hallway, as Neely rushed me into the passenger's seat. "I wasn't anywhere near the bathroom, when yo' momma was bein' all evil and shit, baby. I was getting' a bag packed for you and one for me, so we can get the hell outta here." She said, breathlessly, as she pointed at the bags that sat in the backseat of the car. "Okay, come on Neely, hurry," I exclaimed, as I saw my mother in the doorway of the garage. "Y'all aren't going anywhere!" my mother shrieked. "Get y'all's stupid asses back in the house right now!"

Neely shuffled as quickly as she could around the car to the driver's side, as my mother stomped towards her. "Neely, hurry!" I screamed. My skin was covered in goose bumps and my friends, the ants, began crawling on my scalp once again, making me tingly and nervous as hell. Neely opened the car door as my momma bounded up behind her and slammed it shut, right on Neely's arm. Neely screamed in agony. I looked at her arm, the one that had comforted me so many times. It was now broken, the bone protruding from the skin. "Neely!" I screamed, as I opened my passenger side door, to get out and help her. "Bliss, no baby! Don't get out!" she pleaded, as she pushed her door back open with her left hand, attempting to get into the car. My mother grabbed Neely by the hair, propelling her back into the shelves stacked with gardening tools on the wall. I let out a scream, as tears streamed down my face.

"Bliss, drive baby, go! Get outta here! Go now!" Neely yelled. "I can't leave you here!" I screamed, tears and saliva streaming down my chin. "You have to, Bliss, it's the only way, baby, go now!" Neely pleaded. I scooted across the center console into the driver's seat, as my momma ran towards the car with an axe, that had fallen from the shelf when Neely's body slammed into it. My hands shook like crazy. I didn't have a driver's license. I didn't know how to drive a car. I had ridden in that exact car several times, when I tagged along with Neely on trips to the store. *How the hell do I get this thing to go?* I wondered, as I stepped on the gas pedal. I could hear the engine rev up. "It won't move!" I screamed, as my mother proceeded to bust out the driver's side window. "Pull the handle on the right side down to R, to back out, then D to go forward," Neely yelled breathlessly, as she struggled to stand up. As I found the handle, my mother reached through the broken glass and slammed my head into the steering wheel.

I felt a warm stream trickle from the top of my forehead, down my face. I smelled the unmistakable iron smell. I knew that it was blood. I opened the door hard and knocked my mother down. "Come on Neely, get in!" I pleaded, as she attempted to run to the passenger's side. I saw my mother stand up and grab the axe in her hand. I leaned over and opened the passenger's side door for Neely, knowing that the pain in her arm must be excruciating, at that point. "Jump in, Neely!" I yelled. My mother ran around the front of the car, towards Neely, holding the axe high above her head. *She's gonna kill her,* I thought. I looked over into the passenger's seat, Neely was only halfway into the car. "Hold on tight, Neely," I said, as I slammed the car into reverse and pushed the gas pedal. We pulled out of the garage, hitting, the rod iron fence with the back of the car. "Shut the door, shut the door!" I insisted, looking at Neely. Sweat was pouring down her face. I switched the car into drive and peeled out of the driveway, as Neely slammed her door shut. I glanced into the rearview mirror and saw the woman that had caused me so much emotional pain. I swear, in that moment, I could hear the tiny voices of my spirit guides in my head cheering for me. I was free!

Chapter Eleven

I drove through the neighborhood like Cruella DeVille, fast as lightning and reckless as hell. Once we reached St. Charles Avenue, Neely told me to put the car in park and that she would drive. I pulled the car over to the right side of the road, put it in park, turned my head and looked right at her. "You can't drive with your arm busted up like that," I responded, "I gotta get you to a hospital quick!" Neely looked at me, shook her head and said, "No hospitals, baby. Yo' momma knows that she broke my arm and gashed yo' head open. Soon as she can get all those socialites out of her house without causing a scene, she's gonna head to the hospitals first, lookin' for our asses. I ain't 'bout to let us get caught and dragged back into that hell, no ma'am." I nodded in agreement. Getting caught could not happen. If my mother caught us, she'd kill us for sure.

Neely opened the glove compartment and hastily grabbed some wadded up fast food napkins that she had stored in there from one of our French fries and vanilla shake snack stops. That was our special treat on errand days. Hot, salty fries, with thick vanilla shakes, the kind that are made with real ice cream. That was one of the main reasons that I liked tagging along with Neely on shopping trips, the promise of our special snack, before heading back to the prison that I had lived in my entire life.

Neely continued talking, "Now let's clean yo' head up a bit, girl," she said, as she held the napkins up to her mouth, with her good arm, putting her saliva on them, in order to wet them a bit, before dabbing them on my forehead, where it had been gashed open. Then, she continued, "It's twelve somethin' in the afternoon, and nobody wants to see blood as they are drivin' to go eat them some lunch. Plus, we don't need no po-lice officers gettin' suspicious and pullin' our asses over, ya hear? They'd send our butts right back to Ms. Cecily's house, quicker than snot! She'd tell them that I'd kidnapped ya or some shit, I'm sure of it, with you still bein' a minor and all. Which means, you need to stop drivin' like a bat out of hell, girlfriend! The po-lice be lookin' for drivers like you. Just calm yo' ass down and listen to me." "Where are we gonna go?" I asked frantically, the intensity revving itself up in my veins once again. My skin flushed, as thoughts rolled through my mind. *We have nowhere to go. We can't go to the police. We can't get help. We will be homeless! How will we survive? Did Neely think to bring the coffee can of cash when she packed our bags in a frenzy, during momma's fit earlier?* Neely looked calm. She patted my knee with her one working hand, as she looked into my eyes, calming my nerves, and said, "Don't worry baby girl, I know exactly where we will be safe. Now put the car in drive and let's go."

For the next fifteen minutes, or so, I channeled every bit of focus that I could into listening to Neely's driving directions and being as cautious as I possibly could. I knew that I could not get us pulled over. Our fates depended upon me at that moment. I didn't know where Neely was leading me to, but I trusted her with my life. I knew that she would take care of me. I just hoped that wherever it was that we were going, she could get help with her broken arm. It creeped me out to look at it, so I tried to keep my eyes focused on the road and nothing else. "Okay baby, up here ya gonna take a right, then pull up to the house at the end of the street," Neely advised. I did, just as she said.

When we pulled up to the house, a feeling of comfort surrounded me. It was a small one-story, modest house, painted a deep violet, which made me think of velvet, for some reason. The front porch had two rocking chairs, painted black. In between the rocking chairs, was a square shaped table, adorned with gorgeous oddities. I opened my driver's side door, in order to get out and have a closer look. I was mesmerized by the beauty and the mystery of this house. "I feel like I've been here before, I'm having a very déjà vu moment," I gushed. "You have, sweet pea, you have," Neely replied, with a watered down version of her alligator smile. I knew she must have been in a lot of pain and that she probably was not able to muster up enough energy to give me her full version of the smile that I adored so much. "Let me help you out of the car, Neely," I insisted, as she struggled with her door handle. "Thank you, sweet girl," Neely replied, breathlessly. As I helped her out of the passenger's side, she grunted loudly, trying to get the strength to get her plump body up out of the seat, without putting pressure on her arm. The smell of sulfur wafted through the air, and I knew that the force of Neely's grunt must have made her fart. Normally I would have laughed my ass off, as I did every time that Neely let one rip, which was frequently. Usually when I caught her, she would grin and say something like, "That smell ain't me, Miss Bliss, there must be some deviled eggs around here somewhere." Then we would both laugh until we had tears in our eyes and our stomachs hurt. I knew better than to laugh that time, though I wanted to. Neely was hurting really badly and I knew that if I started laughing, she wouldn't be able to resist the urge to laugh, and it might make her arm hurt worse. Therefore, to keep my giggles from bursting out of my mouth, I used my tried and true technique.

***

I had used it on occasions, when I would think something was funny, but it was inappropriate to laugh. It had come in handy during many of the church services that my mother had made me attend through the years. Don't get me wrong, I respected the sanctity of Christianity. It was just that there was this old woman that seemed to sit in the pew behind us, every single Sunday that I attended. I swear, that woman thought she was a damn opera singer or something. We'd be all standing up, holding our hymnals, singing "How Great Thou Art", and that woman acted like she thought she was performing at the Sydney Opera House. I'm all for being loud and proud, but that woman had no business being either of those things. She had one of those typical old lady voices with way too much vibrato and as shrill as you could possibly get. I do have to give that woman some credit though, she inspired my 'keep it serious' technique. When she would sing, I would just think of the saddest thing that my mind could think of. I would think about the starving children in Africa that I saw on commercials every time that I watched T.V., I would think about homeless people, I would think about puppies trapped in animal shelters, things like that. My technique had not failed me then, and I was glad that it did not fail me as I walked with Neely up towards the alluring mystery house.

***

We made our way up the front walkway, which was glimmering in the midday sunlight. I looked down and noticed that the walkway was made up of different colored crystals, stone, and pieces of colored glass. They were each in deep, rich hues; which added to the allure of the house. I was head over heels in love and I had not yet seen the inside of the home. There was something mystical and magical about the structure that stood before me. It was as if the house itself was not just simply wood and nails, it was as if it had a soul; the kind of soul that you can't help but be attracted to, the kind of soul that's deep, moody, and weird; but in the best possible way. I didn't know what Neely's plan was, but I hoped that we could live there forever. I felt that the house had the power to heal my weary and ragged spirit. It was beckoning me, ready to wrap itself around me and hold me tightly. As we climbed the three steps up to the porch, the front door opened. There, in the doorway stood the most beautiful black woman that I had ever seen. "Well, hello Bliss, hello Neely, I've been waiting for y'all," the woman said, in a voice that was smooth, rich, and as comforting as a nice warm bubble bath.

Chapter Twelve

She was wearing all black, looking both chic and whimsical at the same time. *That's a tough combination to pull off*, I thought, but that woman was owning it, let me tell you. She had on some Audrey Hepburn style cropped pants over what looked like a ballet leotard that had spaghetti straps and ruching at the top, making it into a sweetheart-style neckline. On top, she wore a sheer kimono, that flowed all the way down to her ankles. She was stunning. Tall and thin, with perfect skin, the color of whipped butterscotch icing. She looked to be in her early to mid 40s, if I were to guess. *She's probably around the same age as my mother, but a whole hell-of-a-lot cooler*, I thought. Her dark hair was parted to the side and swept back into a low chignon bun. Her eyes were a light hazel color, and they sparkled in the afternoon sun. *She must've been a ballerina when she was younger*, I concluded. "Miss Dahlia?" I apprehensively presumed. "The one and only," she confirmed with an alluring smile. I caught a glimpse of her teeth. They were a little crooked, not perfect by any means, but they were as white as could be. There was something interesting about them. I liked that they weren't perfectly straight, it gave her character. I hated when people looked too perfect, it made me automatically assume that they were boring. My annoyance of the pursuit of perfection was most definitely derived from the many years of being around my mother and her friends. They were that type to a 'T'. Never a hair out of place, perfectly lined lips, perfectly tailored designer suits, no originality allowed. Creativity scared the hell out of them. To the Cecily Fontaines of the world, individuality meant anarchy and chaos. I knew better than that. People with imperfections and quirks had always been my favorite. Everything about Dahlia and her house exuded the words interesting and intriguing. She definitely had that je ne sais quois.

"Y'all come on inside and I'll get to work on that arm of yours, Neely dahlin'," she started, "If y'all have bags, I'll get 'em later on, let's just get y'all inside for now," she said, as we followed her through the arched doorway into the comfort zone. "I knew ya would know we was comin'," Neely confessed, as she slowly waddled behind Dahlia, holding her broken arm. "You betta believe it, girl," Dahlia replied, "I knew somethin' was brewin' around three this mornin'. I just all of a sudden woke up and got that rush of energy pour over my body that I get when somethin' big is about to happen. So I got up and went to the altar that I have set up in my bedroom. I lit four purple candles, one white candle, and my Virgin of the Guadalupe candle. I sprinkled my frankincense oil on my forehead and I lit my jasmine incense. I was right in the middle of getting' my crystals together, and I mean it, I knew whatever I was about to find out was gonna be big, so I grabbed my strongest crystals. I had purple amethyst, black obsidian, amber, black tourmaline, and sugilite. I was reaching for my malachite when all of a sudden, I saw y'all's names written in the prettiest cursive handwriting, right there in front of my face, just up in the air. I mean, it was crazy, it said, 'Neely and Bliss need you.' That's it. Just that y'all needed me. Crazy, huh?" she asked as we reached her living room. "Yeah, super cra-," I was replying, when she inadvertently interrupted me. She didn't do it in a rude way, it was actually kind of charming. It was as if she was just bursting with excitement to finish the rest of her story that she couldn't wait for me to finish my sentence. Dahlia continued, "I mean, I know Neely, you know, but I don't know if Bliss knows, I mean I see shit all of the time. I mean I get visions and what-not on a daily basis. I'm tellin' y'all, it was crazy though. It was like my spirit guide was writing y'all's names in the air with a Fourth of July sparkler or somethin'. I wish y'all could have seen it." Dahlia said as she helped Neely onto the deep purple, velvet couch. "Lay down now, girl," she told her. "Bliss, why don't you go get yo' self a cup of cold water," she suggested, as she pointed me in the direction of the kitchen. I nodded in agreement.

I was not about to argue with Miss Dahlia. For one, I already adored her. Not in the same way that I adored Neely, it was more like I was in awe of Dahlia. I wanted to be like her. Everything about her was cool. She radiated positive vibes, yet she was mysterious. She was the type of woman that had that presence that commanded a room. She came across the way that I wanted to be seen, positive and happy, with a dash of moodiness. Just enough to say, "hey, I can be the best thing that ever happened to you, or your worst nightmare, your choice."

The other reason that I didn't hesitate to follow Dahlia's instruction to go to the kitchen, was that I knew that she was about to do some hoodoo healing magic on Neely's arm. I wasn't sure what that would entail, but I wasn't sure if I wanted to find out either. Plus, if Miss Dahlia's kitchen was as unique as the rest of her house, I wouldn't mind exploring it a bit.

"Bliss, just help yo'self to anything that you find in there, but if it's in a jar and has a sticker with my handwriting on it, let it be. That's the stuff that I use for my spells. You wouldn't wanna eat or drink most of that shit anyhow!" Dahlia's voice echoed down the narrow hallway that led to the kitchen. "Okay, thanks for the heads up!" I said with a laugh. *Wow, Miss Dahlia is the real deal,* I thought. *She does spells and everything. Maybe, if I'm real sweet, she'll teach me a few.*

As I stepped through the arched doorway into the kitchen, I grinned, pleased with the kitchen décor. The walls were painted a deep, rich shade of red. The kitchen floor was a mosaic of crystals, stones, and colored glass, just like the front walkway. I even noticed some seashells within the mosaic. The tile backsplash was an artwork all on it's own. It was a hodge podge of different jewel toned tiles. Deep blue, purple, emerald green, scarlet, mustard yellow, all randomly placed. There seemed to be absolutely no rhyme or reason to the placement. Miss Dahlia probably liked it like that, not too perfect.

She is the coolest, I thought, as I noticed that the countertops were simply stained concrete slabs. *Oprah needs to know about Miss Dahlia, she could be the new Interior Design guru featured on Oprah's show. Nouveau New Orleans style!*

I made my way towards the stainless steel refrigerator and opened it. It was apparent that Dahlia enjoyed drinking wine. I saw two bottles of pinot grigio, one bottle of chardonnay, three bottles of sauvignon blanc, and one bottle of champagne chilling in the fridge door. Where most people would have ketchup, mustard, mayonnaise, barbecue sauce, and stuff like that, Miss Dahlia only had wine. *She must like to cook, like Neely,* I thought, as I noticed bay leaves, parsley, thyme and lots of other herbs growing in tiny little plant pots near the stained glass window. On the top shelf of the fridge, was a large jug of water marked 'alkaline water' and one marked 'distilled water'. I wasn't completely sure what alkaline water was, or if it was safe to drink, or perhaps an ingredient for one of her spells, so I thought it best to leave it well enough alone. On the other hand, I had read that distilled water was healthy to drink, that it was the purest form of water, so I decided that I would go with that. *Now if I could just find a glass,* I thought. I walked over to the cabinets that were next to the kitchen sink and began opening them. I found the glasses in the second cabinet that I opened.

Even Dahlia's glasses were unique. They each had an image of a tarot card on them. Being superstitious, I decided that I should probably choose my glass carefully. As I looked at all of the beautifully drawn images, my eye was drawn to one in particular, The High Priestess. She was beautiful and intriguing, a lot like Dahlia. I pulled the glass out of the cabinet and began to pour myself a glass of water. It was at that moment that I realized that I had not had anything to drink all day. I had eaten some of Neely's Cajun crabcakes bites before my mother's rant, during the brunch, but I never had the chance to get something to wash it down with, before my momma went postal.

The cold water felt good going down my throat. I drank the entire glass down in two gulps. I poured myself another glass and began to drink it. I sometimes liked to hold the water in my mouth and feel it soak into the inside of my cheeks, before swallowing the rest. I did this several times, finishing off the second glass of water. It was refreshing. I was carefully placing my High Priestess glass into the bottom of the stainless steel sink, when something caught my eye on the other side of the stained glass window that was above the sink. It was something sparkling outside. I couldn't quite make out what it was, due to the beautifully ornate pattern of the stained glass window. After putting the distilled water jug back where it came from, I made my way past the refrigerator towards the back door, in order to get a closer look. Upon opening the back door, I discovered the most fairytale-ish garden I could have ever imagined. Flowers everywhere, adorned with beautiful butterflies and dragon flies flitting to and fro. I stepped onto the stone walkway to get a closer look. The sparkling that I had noticed was from the shimmering water of a small stream that ran through the garden. *Absolutely breathtaking, I thought. This is going to be my favorite reading spot, for sure.* I could just picture myself sitting on the small arched bridge that went over the stream, entranced with the atmosphere and completely immersed in a good novel. I could have sat out in the garden for the rest of the day, getting lost in the beauty and whimsy of it all, but I thought that I better not explore too much. It would probably be best for me to wait and let Dahlia give Neely and I the grand tour. I walked to the back door that lead into the kitchen. As I reached for the doorknob, I caught a glimpse of my reflection in the window of the door. I had forgotten about the gash on my head. It had stopped bleeding, but the dried blood looked nasty as could be. I decided that I should probably go find the bathroom and freshen up.

I could at least attempt to look presentable, being a guest in Miss Dahlia's house and all.

I meandered through the kitchen and back to the narrow hallway that I had traversed from the living room, not five minutes before. I could hear Dahlia chanting and I could smell sage burning. "Oya, Orisha goddess of storms and winds. Our woman warrior, accept this charm as a gift from us, a token of our respect…" I could hear Dahlia saying. I wasn't quite sure what would happen if a healing spell was interrupted, but I sure as hell didn't want to piss off Oya, so I decided to find the bathroom on my own. I walked towards the opposite end of the hallway, noticing an open door on the right. *This must be it*, I decided, as I rounded the corner of the doorway and walked in.

To my surprise, there was a guy standing at the toilet, with his back to me. "Oh my god, I am so sorry!" I said nervously, as I stumbled out of the bathroom, slamming the door shut behind me. *Holy crap,* I thought, as I stood in the hallway, my heart racing. *That scared the shit out of me. I didn't know anyone else was here. I am so embarrassed!* I heard the toilet flush, followed by the sound of the sink water running. I wasn't sure where I should go. Was it weird for me to be waiting in the hallway? Before I could make a break for it, the bathroom door opened, but no one emerged. "Sorry I scared you, my mother didn't tell me we were having company," a voice said. "No, I'm sorry, I didn't know that Miss Dahlia had a son, in fact, I didn't know that anyone else was here. I don't usually just barge into bathrooms like that." I responded. He peeked his head out of the doorway and looked at me with his stunning light green eyes. He was very handsome, he had light brown hair, that looked as if he had just crawled out of bed. His skin was much lighter than Dahlia's, which made me assume that his father was probably white. There was no way that he was adopted, because that guy had the exact same smile and the same teeth as Miss Dahlia. "I'm Mathias," he said, extending his right arm out of the doorway, I extended mine and shook his hand, "Nice to meet you, I'm Bliss," I responded. My skin felt hot, and I could tell that I was blushing. I hoped that it wasn't painfully obvious. "Well Bliss, I'm sorry to have to do this to you, but um, I'm um, just wearing my boxer shorts. Sorry, I mean, if I had known there was someone here besides my momma, I would've gotten dressed. So, if you wanna maybe turn around, I can make a mad dash to my room. Then the bathroom is all yours." Mathias said with a smile. "Yeah, no problem," I said, trying not to sound flustered or nervous. I turned my back to him. "You're good now," I informed him. "Cool, thanks, Bliss," he said, as I heard his footsteps run down the hallway, "gorgeous name, by the way. It suits you." My stomach felt as if all of the butterflies from Miss Dahlia's garden were in it. I turned around and he was nowhere to be seen.

I covered my mouth with my hands as I entered the bathroom. *Had Mathias just flirted with me?* I had never been allowed to socialize with anyone my own age, except for at the Miss New Orleans pageant, but none of them were guys. I hadn't expected to meet a cute guy today, of all days. First, I almost get killed by my mother, then I rescue my best friend, then I drive a car for the first time in my life, without a legal driver's license, I might add; then I arrive at a mystery house, occupied by a mystic hoodoo woman, whom I adore instantly, then I meet her equally charming son. *Could this day get any crazier?* I turned on the sink water to wash the dried blood off of my face. As I searched for a washcloth I cringed, thinking about the fact that Mathias' first impression of me was with my forehead covered with dried blood and tear stains on my cheeks. *Oh yeah, and don't forget about the psycho girl haircut, Bliss. He must think that I am all kinds of weird*, I thought, as I grabbed a black washcloth from the bathroom cabinet next to the tub. I proceeded to wash away the craziness of the day, grinning at myself in the mirror, allowing myself to soak in a moment of happiness, as I pictured the adorable way that Mathias had smiled at me.

Chapter Fourteen

It took me ten minutes or so, but I had managed to make myself somewhat presentable, thanks to the lip gloss, mascara, and rouge that I had managed to find within the bathroom cabinets and drawers. I also discovered a hairbrush and some hairspray, which helped to tame the homeless looking Peter Pan hairdo that I was stuck with until it could grow out enough to look feminine once again. *Please tell me you have some mouthwash stashed away in here, Miss Dahlia,* I hoped. I couldn't locate any, but I did find some toothpaste. I put toothpaste on my index finger and went to town on my chompers. It had only been a couple of hours since I had brushed my teeth that morning at my mother's house, but I felt a sense of release as I scrubbed away all of the sobs and cruel, hateful words, that had left a bitter taste on my tongue. *Hallelujah,* I thought when I discovered a stick of rose scented deodorant and a bottle of pear scented body splash. My sleuthing skills had come in handy once again. I hoped that Miss Dahlia wouldn't mind me using her toiletries. She seemed like the type that would want a guest to make themselves at home and wouldn't make a fuss over a few squirts of body splash coming up missing from her bottle. I took one last glance in the mirror before heading out into the hallway. *Not bad,* I thought to myself, *I clean up pretty good.*

As I stepped off of the tiled bathroom floor, onto the dark, hardwood floor of the hallway, I deliberately coughed. I had no idea where Mathias was in the house, at that point, but I hoped that he would hear my dainty cough and emerge to come and talk to me again. I wanted him to see the somewhat gussied up version of myself. People say that first impressions last forever, I hoped to God that the saying wasn't true. Ten minutes ago, I looked like complete white trash and I wasn't about to let that vision stick in his mind forever. I glanced down the hallway to my right, which was the part of the house that I had not yet ventured into. *His bedroom must be down that way,* I thought. I listened for any signs of life coming from that direction, but all I could hear was the muffled laughter of Neely and Dahlia. *They're laughing? That must mean that Neely's arm is all better.* I couldn't imagine that they would chuckle during a healing ceremony, so I thought that it was probably safe for me to join them. As I turned left and headed down the hallway towards the living room, I glanced behind me, hoping to see Mathias. *You have more pressing matters,* I told myself. *You haven't even asked Dahlia if you and Neely can stay here. If she says no, what the heck are you gonna do? You have nowhere to go. You are not like other girls, Bliss. Other girls your age, have nothing to worry about, besides who is going to take them out on Saturday night and how to achieve the perfect sunless tan, without looking like an Oompa-Loompa. Just worry about yourself, you don't need a guy, at least not right now.*

I was deep in thought, oblivious to the sounds coming from the kitchen as I passed it, making my way to the living room, when I felt a light tap on my shoulder. I jumped as I turned around to see who had caught me off guard. It was him. "Hey, what's goin' on in that pretty head of yours?" he inquired with a mischievous grin. His hair was still disheveled, but he had managed to throw on a grey LSU t-shirt and a black pair of basketball shorts. He was holding a bowl of Fruity Pebbles cereal, which he proceeded to take another bite of, while he waited for my response. I smiled back at him and replied, "I was just trying to figure things out, it's been a long day already." "Already? It's only two in the afternoon, I just woke up like fifteen minutes ago," he said, as he took another bite of cereal. I laughed, "Wow, you're quite the go-getter," I teased, as I turned and continued down the hallway into the living room, where I found Dahlia and Neely drinking wine and talking.

"Hey baby girl, where'd you run off to?" Neely asked, showing her full alligator smile. "I was freshening up. How's your arm?" I asked. "Much better, honey, I'll tell ya what, Dahlia knows her shit!" Neely looked at Dahlia when she said it and they both raised their wine glasses in the air and clinked them together, then they took nice long swigs. "Mmmhmmm, and this is also helpin' to make my arm feel better," she added with a smile. "Glad to hear it," I replied, as I sat down on a bright green ottoman. Dahlia looked at me, sensing the concern on my face. "She's gonna be sore for a day or two, but I reset her arm, and healed her puncture wound. She's got some bruising, but she can use her arm now. Of course, you and me are gonna have to make sure she takes it easy and doesn't lift really heavy things for the next three months, but I think we can manage that together, right Bliss?" she confided with a wink. *She wants us to stay here, at least for a few months*, I thought, as I breathed a sigh of relief. "Yes, we can definitely manage that," I assured, looking right at Dahlia, as I mouthed 'thank you'. She nodded and mouthed 'my pleasure'.

"Bliss, you want some wine, girl?" Dahlia offered as she stood up from the leopard print armchair that she was relaxing in. "Um, I'm only seventeen, I haven't drank before," I replied. She wrinkled her nose, in thought, and said, "That's right, I forgot how young you are child, 'cause your aura is just so sophisticated. You're such an old soul, girl. I mean that as a compliment. I don't like people who act a fool, I like old souls who get 'it', ya know, people who know who they are and who aren't afraid to be that person. Geez, that means it's only been what, thirteen years since you were last here with me?" Dahlia turned and looked at Neely, "she knows, right, Neely? I feel like she knows." "Yep, she knows," Neely confirmed, "I told her awhile back. Actually, Dahlia, Miss Bliss is 'bout to be eighteen, can ya believe it? Next month will be fo'teen years since that night. I can't believe it. Fo'teen years since she was here. I'll tell ya Dahlia, I jus'…" Neely was interrupted. "That was you?" Mathias' voice echoed from the hallway as he emerged through the archway into the living room, still holding his bowl of cereal. "Mathias!" Dahlia beamed, as she ran over to him and embraced him with a hug. "Hi Mom," he said with a grin. "When did you get here?" she inquired, as she put her hands on the sides of his face, took a step back and looked at him. "I had a final at five yesterday that lasted until around eight. By the time I got back to the dorm and finished packing up all of my stuff, it was around eleven thirty or so, and I didn't want to risk waking you up by calling, so I thought, 'what the hell', I might as well come on home, instead of waiting 'til morning." he answered. "I'm so glad my baby boy is home for the summer!" she gushed. *How cute, she still calls him her baby boy,* I thought. I looked at Mathias, with a giant smile on my face and I raised my eyebrows. He smiled back and blushed. It felt good to be able to tease him a little bit, it felt like we were friends who had known each other for years, we just flowed. I liked that he 'got' it. He knew what I meant by the smile and the eyebrow raise. I didn't have to explain myself. *He 'gets' me.*

"Oh, how incredibly rude of me," Dahlia continued, "Neely, Bliss, this is my son, Mathias. Mathias, that's Neely, and that's Bliss, all grown up now, can you believe it? You remember when she was just a lil' thing, like three or four, wasn't she, Neely?" Neely nodded, "yep, she was fo'." Dahlia looked back at Mathias and said, "Remember when she was here for those few days and you and her played in the garden, catchin' ladybugs and roly polys during the day and fireflies at night? Oh y'all were so cute! Yeah, that's right, she was four, because I remember, you were six years old, Mathias. That was the summer after you had just finished kindergarten. You were so happy to have a lil' friend over for a few days, 'cause man alive, you didn't make hardly any friends in kindergarten." "Thanks Mom," Mathias said, with a chuckle, then he looked right at me, widened his light green eyes, pointed at his mother and shook his head, as if to say 'can you believe this woman?' The butterflies inhabited my stomach once again. I felt a connection with him already and I loved it. Dahlia nudged Mathias, and continued her story, "Oh, you know I didn't mean nothin' bad by that, son. You were just on a whole 'nother level than the other kids in your class, that's all. They were all eatin' paste and there you were, makin' art work that could be displayed in the New Orleans Museum of Art. I know, I know, I'm probably just a little bit biased because you are my one and only. Let me just tell you though, I am proud that you ended up being more social as you grew up." "Thanks Mom," Mathias snickered, as he leaned over and gave Dahlia a kiss on her cheek. He was tall. I had been so flustered during our earlier encounter that I had not noticed his height. Miss Dahlia was taller than me by at least four or five inches, easy. She had that long and lean, dancer type body, the one that all men love and all women would kill to have. She must have been around five foot nine or five foot ten, and yet Mathias still had to lean over to kiss his mother on the cheek. *He's gotta be six foot two, at least,* I thought. He had that build that wasn't 'meat head style' muscular, but that was toned enough to make any girl feel safe with him. I shivered as a tingle of excitement coursed through my body. "You cold, Bliss?" Miss Dahlia asked, "I can bump the air up a bit, honey." she offered as she rubbed my arms with her hands. I nodded and falsely accused the A/C of being the reason for my shiver. I was not about to let anyone, especially Mathias, in on the truth. Dahlia walked towards the thermostat that was mounted on the living room wall, near the hallway. She adjusted the temperature as she continued talking, "Neely and Bliss will be staying here with us for awhile, Mathias. So, honey, if you wouldn't mind gettin' the guest room ready for them, it would help me out a lot." Mathias had just taken another bite of his 2 p.m. breakfast, so he just nodded and gave her a thumbs up as he turned to go get started. "Oh and honey, first, you need to go take a shower. Remember, we have a gorgeous young lady in the house now." Dahlia said, as she looked at me and winked. Mathias kept walking and held up his right arm giving her another thumbs up.

"Alright ladies, before we can chill, there are a few more things that we need to take care of," Dahlia started, " let me grab y'all's car keys and I can move Mathias' car out of the garage and I'll put y'all's car in there, just in case yo' momma has notified the police to be on the lookout for the car. We don't need no one bustin' in and ruining our big plans. Nope, there is too much at stake. Bliss baby, you've got yourself one big and amazing life ahead of you to live, and I am certainly not going to risk your fate gettin' all messed up on account of me sittin' on my fine ass drinking me some pinot grigio, being too lazy to hide a damn car in a garage. So if y'all will just point me in the direction of the keys, I will get to it." I adored Dahlia, she was awesome. The way she worded things, made everything sound witty and cool, I hoped that one day I could be just like her. I pointed to the side table near the couch, "I laid them over there," I reported. "Great," Dahlia exclaimed, as she grabbed the keys, "Bliss, would you go ask Mathias for his car keys for me, please? He probably went off to his room to grab some clean britches to take with him to the bathroom to put on after he scrubs up. Just go down the hallway and his bedroom is the last door on the left. When you get his car keys, just go through the kitchen and out the back door. If you walk to the back left corner of the garden, there's a small gate in the white picket fence. Just reach yo' hand over the gate and you'll feel a little latch. It shouldn't be locked, so just open that sucker and you can come on out onto the driveway to bring me his keys. Just meet me out there, okay? I'm gonna pull y'all's car around." She didn't wait for me to answer, she just walked out the front door.

I turned to head towards the hallway, when I heard Neely say, "We're gonna be alright now, baby." I turned back around, ran over to Neely and hugged her. I was careful not to touch her sore arm. "I love you, Neely," I gushed. "I love ya too, baby girl, I love ya too," she whispered as she patted my back. "Damn girl, you be smellin' good! What is that? Pears or somethin'? Dang, that smells good, girl! Who you tryin' to impress?" Neely teased as she widened her eyes, raised her eyebrows, and shot me a grin. I felt my ears get hot and I knew that my face had probably turned a lovely shade of crimson. "None ya," I replied with a laugh. 'None ya' was kind of an inside joke between Neely and myself. It had been a phrase that I had heard Neely use ever since I was little. It was short for 'none ya damn business' she had told me.

***

The phrase had especially come in handy throughout the years when I would tag along with her on trips to the grocery store and what not. People would stare at us like we were circus freaks, probably wondering what a porcelain skinned blonde girl was doing with a 'large and in charge' black woman. If I had a dime for every time someone had stopped us and asked me if I was okay, I swear I'd be able to buy about ten yachts. Every time someone would question us, Neely would respond with, "none ya." Of course, it was always the hoity toity old money type that would approach us, we did most of our shopping in the Garden District, therefore, we were constantly surrounded with the same high cotton type of people. I always thought it was hilarious when they would wrinkle their brows and ask Neely what she said. Neely would mutter, "it means none ya damn business, so go on and get on." I had never understood their questioning. *Of course I was okay, I was with the only person in the entire world that cared for me.* When I was little, I would always ask Neely what the people had meant by their questions. She always had the same response, she'd say, "Bliss, some people are just ignorant fools, honey, you can't fix stupid." I would just shrug my shoulders and accept her answer, although I was still all kinds of confused. When I was about twelve or thirteen, she finally sat me down and explained it to me after some man had the audacity to stop us right in the middle of our grocery shopping and accuse Neely of kidnapping me. Can you believe it? He seriously, God's honest truth, believed that Neely was some kind of criminal who had taken me for ransom, or some shit. *Rich people, I swear!* I remember we were in the produce section, picking out some green tomatoes, that Neely was going to fry up with supper, when this overweight, middle aged, bald headed man walks right up in between Neely and I. "Young lady, why don't you come with me and we can get you to your parents," he'd said. "I beg your pardon?" I'd replied. "Excuse you, mister big headed bigot!" Neely shouted, "I'd like to know just what kind of bull shit you are tryin' to pull, mister. C'mon Bliss, let's get away from this racist asshole before his disgusting mindset rubs off on us." As Neely grabbed my hand to lead me away from the man, he grabbed her forearm forcefully and told her, in words that I cannot even bear to utter, that she needed to leave me the 'you know what' alone and that he had already called the police to report the kidnapping. I tried explaining to him that she was my mother's maid and that I was just tagging along to help her do the shopping. He kept saying, "I know that black woman told you to lie, darlin', but you're safe now, the police are gonna be here any minute, you can tell the truth." Neely was mad as hell and seeing red. She called that man every bad name that you could think of. I kept trying to tell her to calm down, I knew that if she was raising cane when the police arrived, it would just make her look like the bad guy. Neely could not be calmed down, she was livid. I swear she would've knocked that jerk into next week, had the police not walked up when they did. The officers took down both sides of the story, and although they listened as Neely told her side, it was painfully obvious that they did not believe one single word that Neely said. They kept kind of brushing her off and asking the man, 'what *really* happened'. My little pre-teen self had never imagined that my best friend, my care giver, Neely, whom I loved and adored more than anyone else in the world, could be treated this way. I remember my anger intensifying as the so-called questioning continued. Were they treating Neely this way because she was black or because she was a woman? *Maybe both*, I thought. I wasn't sure, but either way, I knew it was wrong and I was fuming.

New Orleans' Finest, were once again, listening to the jerk talk out of his ass, when I interrupted him mid-sentence. "Shut up, asshole!" I yelled. I had never said a cuss word before. I had heard Neely say them all of the time, but I knew that she would not approve of me talking like that, heck I was only twelve or thirteen and as naïve as could be. To tell the truth, I shocked the hell out of myself when those words flew out of my mouth, but I couldn't let my surprise or my fear show. Heck no, I was gonna stand my ground. *Nobody is gonna treat my Neely like that*, I thought. "Excuse me, young lady, did I hear you right?" the asshole asked, looking shocked as hell. "Damn straight you heard me right!" I continued. "Young lady, I am just trying to help you get away from this dangerous woman. That's why I called the police. Women like her are often desperate for money, so they turn to kidnapping for ransom. Trust me, young lady, this woman knows that this is a very wealthy area of New Orleans. She knows exactly what she is doing. She is no fool, young lady." he replied. "You're right about one thing, she is most definitely not a fool. I guarantee you that she is smarter than your ivy league educated ass. You sir, are the foolish one. I am not in danger," I fumed. He laughed in the most 'oh you're just a child, you have no idea what you're talking about' kind of way, which made my skin crawl. There is probably nothing that I detest more than someone, especially a man like that, belittling someone else. At that point in my life, I had not yet experienced it first-hand. That day, in the produce aisle of the supermarket, in front of dozen of curious onlookers, who had nothing better to do than watch a pre-teen girl tell off a man that was four times her age, that day, I decided that I was not going to stand for it. Never. I told myself that I would never let a man make me feel like my thoughts and feelings didn't matter. My pale skin got heated and flushed, as my frustration grew. The ignorant man responded, "Then, I suppose you would be happy to inform me and these fine officers of the reason that you are here at this establishment with this woman." I stared daggers right into his eyes and replied, "None ya." "I beg your pardon? What exactly is that?" he asked, looking at the police officers. They shrugged their shoulders, curious as to the meaning of the statement as well. The audience began whispering to one another, probably trying to figure out the meaning of my statement. I made no expression, I continued to stare at the man, narrowing my eyes, as I continued, "I said, none ya. It is short for 'none ya damn business." The man looked right at me and chuckled. Bad move on his part, as this added fuel to my already smoldering fire. That's when I went off, saying, "where the hell do you think you get off treating us this way? You think you're all high and mighty and that you know everything. I'm telling you right now; and officers, feel free to take this down in y'all's notebooks; you, mister, are nothin' but a misogynistic racist! This woman here," I said, as I pointed at Neely, "takes care of me. Hell, she is more of a mother to me than my own mother is, way more! She is not kidnapping me. It is sad that just because she is black and I am white, you automatically assume that I'm in danger. I feel sorry for you, mister. You obviously don't know shit about real life."

Once I had finished my soapbox rant, reality sunk in. I wasn't sure if I would be in trouble with the police for going off like I did. Everyone just stared at me, with wide-eyed, stunned expressions on their faces. I looked at Neely for guidance on what I should do at that point. She flashed her alligator smile and started cracking up laughing, which made the police officers laugh. "Wow girl, you're a little firecracker!" one of the officers commented, "good for you for putting us all in our places. It's refreshing to see a youngster have some guts nowadays. I think we're done here," he said, looking at his partner. His partner nodded with a smile. "Have a nice day, ma'am," he said to Neely. Then he looked at the jerk of a man and told him to find another store to shop in.

***

My big moment that day in the grocery store had made "none ya", a running joke between Neely and myself, which made it the perfect response to her questions about me getting gussied up. I knew that she knew that it was for Mathias' benefit, but I wasn't about to admit that to her. "I better go get those keys from Mathias before he gets in the shower," I said, as I walked quickly out of the living room into the hallway. My heart pounded as I made my way to the last door on the left, the one that Dahlia had said was Mathias' room. The door was closed, so I raised my right fist up to knock. I was shaking, nervous that I would say something embarrassing in front of him. Before my fist could hit the wood, the door opened. I jumped, startled. "Oh hey," Mathias said. "Hey!" I replied hoarsely. I cleared my throat and started again, "hey your mom wanted me to come and ask you for your car keys. She wants to move your car out of the garage and put Neely's in there instead." "Okay, no problem," he replied. "You can go grab them, if ya want. They are over on my desk somewhere," he said, as he brushed past me and headed down the hallway towards the bathroom. "Will do, thanks!" I babbled, as I stepped into Mathias' threshold.

Chapter Fifteen

Mathias' room was tidy and organized, except for the unmade bed. I wondered if the cleanliness had been Miss Dahlia's doing or his. *Is Mathias a neat freak or has he not yet had a chance to dishevel the room, since he's been home for less than twenty four hours?* I wondered. There was an LSU flag hanging on the wall above his bed, a bulletin board with a few concert tickets and scraps of paper with phone numbers scribbled on them tacked up, and some shelves with trophies and various sports memorabilia. Propped against the wall, next to Mathias' bed, was an acoustic guitar. I wondered if he knew how to play or if it was just for decoration. On one wall of the bedroom, stood a nice, tall, cedar bookshelf that had five shelves packed with books. I wanted to see what kind of books he owned. You can tell a lot about a person by what types of books they read. I hoped his were interesting novels and not something cheesy, or simply textbooks that he was required to have for his college classes. I hoped he read for pleasure, like I did.

I started to walk towards the bookshelf to investigate, but I remembered that Miss Dahlia was waiting for me out by the garage. She seemed like a patient woman, but I didn't want to test her patience, especially not on the day of my arrival. Miss Dahlia was kind enough to let Neely and myself stay with her and I was not willing to jeopardize that opportunity. I noticed the desk that Mathias had spoke of, tucked into the far corner of his bedroom, near the window, which overlooked the garden. As I approached the desk, I noticed a framed picture of him with his arms around a girl. *Does he have a girlfriend?* I wondered, as I felt my stomach drop. I had no right to be upset about it, I knew that. After all, I had just met Mathias. It was my fault for mistaking his kindness for flirting. *Maybe he's just charming to everyone,* I thought. *Maybe he was just being extra nice to me because he feels sorry for me. He feels sorry for me.* That thought made my stomach hurt. I shook my head, trying to free myself from the negative feelings of self-doubt that had emerged. As I leaned in to get a better look at the girl in the photograph, a loud ringing sound startled me. I jumped back, my heart pounding. I looked at his desk and found the source of the scare. There, in the back corner of his desk, was a mobile phone with a cord plugged into it. The cord was connected to a plug that was plugged into an outlet next to his desk. I had not seen a mobile phone in real life, only on commercials. They had just become more mainstream and manageable about two years earlier, in 1998. Prior to that, they had been ridiculously huge and expensive, only Wall Street types carried them around. A lot of people still had pagers in lieu of cellular phones, but the popularity was definitely spreading. I hoped that one day I could have a mobile phone of my own. It made sense that Mathias had one, being in college and all. The phone had stopped ringing and I heard a faint 'ding' sound. I wasn't sure what that meant.

Back to the task at hand, I thought, as I located Mathias' keys. As I turned to head out of the room, I was startled once again as Mathias' mobile phone began ringing. I glanced at the front screen of the phone and it said, 'Jennifer Home'. *Jennifer,* I thought. *I wonder if that is the girl in the picture's name.* I leaned in to get a look at the photograph. "Shit, sorry, I thought you had already gotten the keys," Mathias' voice blurted, scaring the crap out of me. I whipped around, hoping he didn't notice that I was looking at the picture. He was standing in the doorway of his room with nothing on but a bath towel wrapped around his waist. "I forgot my shaving cream," he announced, gesturing towards his open duffel bag that sat at the foot of his bed. I tried to look away, to look at anything but him, at that moment.

His cellular phone had stopped ringing and it made the 'ding' sound once again. "Uh yeah, I found them, thanks," I muttered, nervously. As I took a step towards the door, his mobile phone started ringing again. "Will you go look at the screen and tell me who it is?" he asked. It was the third call within the past forty five seconds. I knew who it was, Jennifer, but I certainly was not going to let him know that I had snooped. I leaned over the phone and said, "it says, 'Jennifer Home'." With that I walked out of the room.

As I made my way down the hallway towards the kitchen, I heard Mathias' voice echo as he answered the call, "Hey you," he said, "yeah I was just about to jump in the shower. Nothin' much, just woke up a little while ago and that's about it…" His voice faded out of earshot as I walked through the kitchen and out the back door. *Nothin' much, just woke up a little while ago and that's about it,* echoed through my mind. *It's weird that he wouldn't say anything about his mom having two refugees randomly show up at the house to stay for, Lord knows how long. Why wouldn't he mention that to her? Bliss, stop over analyzing. Don't be 'that' girl,* I told myself.

"Dang girl, glad I wasn't waitin' on the keys to save my life," I heard Dahlia say, as I unlatched the gate in the white picket fence that surrounded the garden. She was standing next to Neely's car, that she had already pulled up the driveway. "Sorry, 'bout that," I replied, "it took me a few minutes to find the darn things." I fibbed. Dahlia smiled at me and said, "I'm just teasin' ya, sweetie, no biggie. Now go on in the door right there on the side of the garage and push the red button to open the big door fo' me. Then you can go ahead and back Mathias' car on out of the garage so I can pull this one in." "Um, I don't really know how to drive, though, so you might wanna be the one to back it up." I told her. "What the --?" Dahlia started. "Girl, how can you be sayin' that you don't know how to drive? I saw ya drive up earlier today with Neely." I chuckled and replied, "yeah that was out of necessity, she couldn't drive with her broken arm, so I had to. I really don't know how." Dahlia pursed her lips together and shook her head at me, "well first thing tomorrow, I'm givin' you driving lessons. I'm not gonna have you not knowing how to drive, girl! You gotta be able to be an independent woman! If you grow up and you are not able to drive yo'self anywhere your little heart desires to go, then what the hell did all the women before us fight for, huh? If you grow up and yo' ass is totally dependent upon a man to even go to the gosh darn store, girl that's just crazy. That ain't happenin'! I will teach you how to drive. You, Miss Bliss, are gonna be an independent woman. That, right there, my dear, is all the 'necessity' you need. Now go on and open the garage fo' me, please ma'am." I beamed at Dahlia, she winked at me, pulled some big cat-eye style sunglasses that she had resting on her head, down over her eyes, sauntered towards me, and gently grabbed Mathias' keys from my hand. I don't know what came over me, but at that moment, I couldn't resist, I wrapped my arms around her and hugged her tightly. My eyes filled with tears, as I whispered, "thank you." Then I turned and made my way to the garage door.

Chapter Sixteen

The afternoon was spry and fleeting. The time passed quickly with Miss Dahlia giving Neely and I an exclusive 'grand tour' of her home and garden, while Mathias carried our bags in and prepared the guest room for us. Before we knew it, seven o'clock had rolled around. That's the thing about summer, it stays light until eight or eight thirty. We hadn't realized the hour, Miss Dahlia and Neely were enjoying their third glasses of pinot grigio, I was on my second glass of Dr. Pepper, and Mathias was sipping on an Abita beer, which he had me hesitantly taste. That boy was convincing, I'll tell ya what. *He could convince Alanis Morissette to sing country music and Dolly Parton to go goth.* I wondered if he always got what he wanted. He seemed like the type of person who did. Not that he was bratty or anything, he was just charming as hell. I wondered if

Jennifer realized the charisma her boyfriend had. *I bet you she does, I thought, that's probably the reason she had her 'creeper status' on level ten earlier, calling his cell phone three times in a row. Who does that? Insecure girls, that's who.* I didn't know a single thing about being in a relationship, but I decided, right then and there, that I never wanted to be a girl like that; a girl that had nothing better to do than to blow her boyfriend's phone up. *It's like, call, leave a message, he'll call you back when he can, geez. Desperate, much?* My thoughts were interrupted when Dahlia looked at the clock on the wall in the living room, jumped up from her leopard print chair, and exclaimed, "would ya look at that? It's already two minutes 'til seven, and I ain't even thought about dinner! Y'all keep on visitin' and I'll whip somethin' up." "Nope," Mathias' voice cut in, "momma, you sit on down and visit, I'll handle dinner." Dahlia smiled and sat right back down as instructed. "Thank you, baby boy," she replied.

He was bored talking to me, he wanted a reason to leave the room, my precarious mind told me. I hoped that wasn't the reason. Thankfully, my mind was put in check when Dahlia looked at me and said, "Bliss, you are in for a real treat, we all are. Mathias is an amazing cook. I told him he should go to culinary school, but that boy has LSU pulling on his heart strings, you know how that goes." I looked down at the bubbles dancing around in my glass and nodded. I just knew she must be talking about Jennifer. Ugh, Jennifer. The name left a bitter taste in my mouth. She's ruining the name, I thought. There are plenty of Jennifers that I'm sure are very awesome and cool people that I would love to hang out with and become BFFs with, but not her. Mathias had only had time to drink about half of his beer before he went to the kitchen, so neither him nor Miss Dahlia had brought up anything about her. Heck, they had no clue that I had done my sleuthing and pieced everything together. I knew that it was foolish for me to be jealous, but I was and I didn't care. I didn't even know the girl and I didn't like her. I know that it is not logical or even morally right to hate someone before you know them, but so what, I knew I didn't like Jennifer and I never would. *Lord, forgive me, but you're just gonna have to give me this one, please,* I thought. As the thoughts were whirling through my mind, I heard the murmur of Neely and Dahlia chit chatting. "Bliss, did ya hear that?" Neely asked. "Huh?" I responded. "Mathias studies at the LSU College of Music and Dramatic Arts. He's a music major. Pretty nifty, right? You and him could go to school together in the fall." Neely said. "Oh that would be wonderful!" Dahlia chimed in. "Yeah, Bliss here, got accepted at Louisiana State University, The University of Texas, and New York University. She's one smart cookie." Neely bragged. I blushed and looked back down at my Dr. Pepper, as I muttered, "Neely, I'm not gonna be able to go to college. I never was. You know momma wouldn't have let me, anyway. I just applied because you encouraged me to. I knew it wasn't gonna happen, and now it's even more unattainable. We don't have money, Neely. Do you realize how expensive college is? Oh that's right, you never went to college, so you don't have a clue." As the hateful words left my lips, I immediately wished that I had a fishing pole to reel them back in with. I knew I shouldn't have said it. Hell, it wasn't Neely's fault that she didn't go to college. She got dealt a hardship of a childhood. Neely had rarely spoken of her upbringing, the few details that I knew were from what she had confided in me when I was around eleven years old.

***

I remembered that day as if it had just happened. Neely was teaching me about the Renaissance and Reformation period of English literature. She was talking about the Early Tudor period when she began reciting some of Edmund Spenser's poetry from memory. I remember being mystified by Neely's knowledge of art and culture. She was an intelligent woman. You would never have guessed just how intelligent Neely was, by just talking to her. She had one hell of a Cajun infused, southern slang accent, but Lordy be, that woman was astute with a capital 'A'. She had been right in the middle of reciting Spenser's work, when my big mouth blurted out one of the most insensitive questions that I had ever uttered. "Gosh Neely, you are smart. You could have been a professor or something. Doesn't it make you sad that you have wasted your life being a maid?" At that time, being only eleven years old, it was the first time that I had felt like I was in desperate need for a rod and reel to take back the harsh words that poured out of my mouth with an unsettling ease. Neely's glittering eyes looked at me, tears welling up in the corners of them, as she calmly replied, "Well Miss Bliss, I don't consider my life wasted, as I get the pleasure of teaching you. Yes, I will admit that my life's ambition was not to be a maid, but what's done is done, and there ain't nothin' I can do 'bout it now. Bliss baby, I don't think I ever told ya, but my daddy was killed when I was just six years old, God rest his soul. He was a butler for a wealthy white man named Luther Chauvin. My daddy was a good butler, from what my momma told me, but daddy also wasn't one to take no shit, neither. Ya know what I'm sayin'?" I remember my little eleven year old head just nodding away, urging Neely to continue. She had never opened up to me about anything from her childhood before that day, and I was anxious to hear more.

"So anyways, Mr. Chauvin and some of his buddies decide that they are gonna go for a weekend duck hunt at some fancy schmancy huntin' lodge 'bout two hours from here. My daddy usually had the weekends off. That was my time with daddy. But you know how spoiled ass people act like they gotta be waited on hand and foot, like they can't do nothin' for themselves. So Luther Chauvin told my daddy that he needed to come along on the trip. I begged my daddy not to go. I had a bad feelin' 'bout the whole thing. I knew Mr. Chauvin had a temper, my daddy had come home with a bloody lip and a black eye at least a few times, that I saw. Momma said that it was because daddy wasn't gonna be treated like dirt, and he let Mr.

Chauvin know it." I interrupted Neely, "Mr. Chauvin hit your daddy?" Neely frowned and nodded her head. "Why did he work for that horrible man? Why didn't he just quit?" I asked, naively. Neely patted my knee and sighed, "Baby, I wish he had, but my daddy was raised to make a commitment and stick with it, no matter how hard it got. Hell, I think my daddy saw it as a challenge to make himself a better person or somethin'. He saw everything as an opportunity for self improvement. I also think he was tryin' to make a good example for us kids, tryin' to show my brother and me that quittin' was not an option, I don't know. Hell you could ask the same thing about me now. Why do I stay and work for yo' crazy momma? I hope ya know that the answer to that question will always be you, Bliss. I stay here for you.

Anyways, my momma used to beg my daddy to quit, but daddy said that he wasn't a quitter and that as long as the money Mr. Chauvin was payin' him kept a roof over our heads and food on our table, that he was gonna ride it out. I'll never forget seeing my daddy get into the black car that Mr. Chauvin had sent to our house to pick him up to go on that duck hunt. I stood outside on our front porch and waved as they drove away, until the car was the size of a crumb. All weekend long, I was just readin' and drawin', waitin' to see my daddy on Sunday evenin'. We couldn't afford much, hell we didn't even have a telephone for my daddy to call us on, so all I could do was wait and try to occupy my time with books and art."

I continued to sit quietly, listening intently to Neely's account of a pivotal moment in her childhood. I didn't dare change the subject, although I had a feeling that what she was getting ready to convey, was not going to be pleasant. Neely continued, "I went out onto the front porch around five o'clock that Sunday evenin', just waitin' on my daddy. He had told my momma that he should be home before suppertime. A couple of hours passed, and still no sign of the black car. The sun set and the moon made its cameo, and still no sign of my daddy. Momma came out onto the porch several times, askin' me to come on in the house. She looked scared to death, Bliss, I'll tell ya, I think she must've thought somethin' bad had happened, but she didn't wanna scare me. I refused to go inside, I wanted to be the first thing my daddy saw when he got home. My brother, Jensen, was twelve years old, at the time. He came out onto the porch for a little while, just waitin' with me. He was tryin' to act like he wasn't worried, for my benefit, I suppose, but I could see the fear written all over his face. After awhile, he told momma that he was gonna go walk to his friend's house to use the phone. He was gonna call the Chauvin residence to see if maybe daddy was just stuck at their house, waitin' on Mr. Chauvin to put his scotch down long enough to have his driver bring daddy home. After Jensen headed down the street, my mother begged me to come on in the house. She kept tellin' me that Jensen would handle it. I refused to leave that front porch." Neely paused, as she took a stifled breath.

She chewed on the inside of her mouth, probably trying to keep from crying in front of me. Then she continued, "Momma knew how stubborn and hard headed I could be, so she brought out a blanket, wrapped it around my shoulders and sat there with me, on our front porch all night long." I interrupted, "What about Jensen? Did he get a hold of your father on the phone?" Neely shook her head, "Nope. He said he called the Chauvin house over and over and nobody answered the phone. When the sun started peekin' up from the horizon, my momma said, 'Neely, Jensen, get y'all's shoes on, we gotta go to Mr. Chauvin's house. I swear, if yo' daddy was too lazy to bring his ass home to his wife and kids last night, and he slept there, I'm gonna whoop his ass! Here we are, sittin' all night long on our front porch, waitin' for his ass. Gettin' all ate up by mosquitoes. Hell no! He better hope I don't find him over there!' I knew, Bliss, I mean I could just sense that momma really did hope that daddy was at Mr. Chauvin's house. 'Cause I think momma knew that if he wasn't, somethin' bad must've happened." Neely paused for a moment, as she reached down the neckline of her blouse and pulled a tissue out of her bra. Neely always stashed things that she might need in her bra. I used to tease her, calling her bra her 'over shoulder everything on God's green earth, holder', instead of the normal 'over shoulder boulder holder'. Neely dabbed the inside corners of her eyes with the tissue, as she took a ragged breath, and commenced her story.

"So momma, Jensen, and I walked the four miles to Mr. Chauvin's house. Believe it or not, back then, I was a skinny little thing. My legs were like little ol' toothpicks. I swear, I thought my legs were gonna break off during that long ass walk. My sweet brother carried me the last half of the way. We didn't have a car. Daddy usually took the bus to the outskirts of Mr. Chauvin's neighborhood, then he would walk about a half of a mile to the house for work every weekday. I thought that was what momma and us was gonna do, but nuh uh, momma said she didn't know the 'damn bus schedule' and that we wasn't gonna be standing at the bus stop for an hour waitin', when we could just walk there ourselves. It took us a long while, but we finally made it to Luther Chauvin's house. It was a beautiful mansion, in this same neighborhood. That house was off of Magazine Street, that's why I never like to drive by that way when you and I go to the store and stuff, Bliss." *Ah ha*, I thought. I had always wondered why Neely avoided a certain block of the Garden District. She would go the long way around, if she had to. When I had asked her in the past her reason for avoiding it, she had always told me that there were too many potholes on that block.

Neely continued, "So my momma rang the doorbell, and Mr. Chauvin, himself answered the door. We had met Mr. Chauvin one time when my daddy was the butler for Mr. Chauvin's Christmas party and we thought that we had been invited as guests. It turned out that Mr. Chauvin's housekeeper had fallen ill, so he wanted momma and us kiddos to fill in for free. That damn cheapskate! So anyways, his fat ass answers the door and momma is just shocked, she doesn't say a word, so I pipe up and ask him where my daddy is. Mr. Chauvin doesn't even invite us to go inside the damn house, he just proceeds to tell us that there was an unfortunate hunting accident and that my father was dead." Neely's voice cracked as she murmured the last sentence. She pulled another tissue out of her bra, wiped her eyes, and blew her nose. I put my skinny little eleven year old arm around her and laid my head on her shoulder. "I'm so sorry, Neely," I whispered. "Thank you, baby," she said. "I mean, can you believe that he gave us no explanation, no further information, nothin'? He just told us that and closed the dang door right in our faces. My momma kept ringin' the bell, as Jensen banged on the glass, but that man would not answer. Momma held us tight and I cried harder than I ever have, Bliss. I swear, I thought that I was going to die. My momma tried to comfort us, but we just sobbed and sobbed, right there on that murderer's front porch. I wanted to bust down that door and kill his ass. I just knew that it hadn't been no accident. That man had a temper, he had hit my daddy before when daddy wouldn't act like a slave for him. I just knew that Luther Chauvin had killed my daddy, but I was a helpless, six year old little girl, I couldn't do nothin' about it."

I chimed in, "Y'all should've told the police, they could've investigated, done somethin' to get that mean man thrown in prison." Neely just shook her head, "Baby, we tried. We sure did try. Straight from that mansion, momma, Jensen, and I walked our tired, bewildered selves to the closest po-lice station. We told the po-lice what had happened. They even brought Mr. Chauvin in for questionin'. They also sent some officers out to the huntin' grounds, two hours away, to investigate. They found nothin'. My daddy was gone, gone for good, without a trace. To tell ya the truth, I wouldn't doubt it if Mr. Chauvin paid to get the whole thing covered up. That man was a millionaire and had friends in high places. There was nothin' that my momma could do. My momma couldn't afford to dwell on it, she had to get a job, to support us. She started cleanin' houses for money. She didn't make much, but it kept a roof over our heads and food in our bellies, it also allowed her to take us with her on cleanin' jobs, when I wasn't in school. That lady worked hard, sometimes she would clean five houses a day, and be tired as could be. I think that's why she died at a young age. She worked herself to death. She died when I was fourteen years old, Bliss. She just got real sick and never got better, poor momma. To tell ya the truth, she may have died of a broken heart. She started getting' sick the day that she found out that my brother had accepted condolence money from Luther Chauvin's widow. I had nothin' against Mrs. Chauvin, for all I knew, she was a nice woman who had married a cold blooded killer. When Luther Chauvin died of liver failure, I was ten years old. His widow, Mrs. Chauvin had come to our house and offered momma money for all of the grief that our family had been put through. My momma was a prideful woman, and she hated Mr. Chauvin. She told his widow that she didn't want any of their filthy money. Mrs. Chauvin had tried a few more times, over the next two years, but momma stuck to her guns. The last time that I saw Widow Chauvin was Christmas Day, when I was twelve years old. Jensen was eighteen and a senior in high school. Mrs. Chauvin obeyed my momma's wishes, promising us that she would leave our family alone. As she left, she told us that if we ever were in need of finances, we were welcome to visit her at her house. My momma yelled at her, tellin' her where that fancy lady could stick her guilty money, as Mrs. Chauvin drove off. It broke my momma's heart, the following spring, when Jensen confessed that he had visited Mrs. Chauvin, and that she was going to pay for his college education, and that she had given him enough money to keep him livin' a fancy-schmancy lifestyle for years to come. That's when my momma fell ill. It tore her apart that Jensen had taken that dirty money. She made me promise her that I would never take money from that woman, that I would earn an honest livin'."

Neely dabbed at her eyes, before continuing, "My momma, she was a good woman. When she passed, I just took over the cleanin' of the houses that she did and took care of myself. I was in the ninth grade and I had to quit school to clean those dad gum houses. I had to, so I could make enough money to survive. If I hadn't, they would've put me in an orphanage. I wasn't 'bout to go down like that. But anyways, that's 'nuff 'bout my childhood, for one day. I got off on a tangent. My point of tellin' ya all of that, Bliss, was so you'd understand why I didn't have the luxury of gettin' a higher education and makin' somethin' of myself. That's the reason I 'wasted my life', as ya put it. Although, I wouldn't want to be doin' nothin' else, besides takin' care of you." I was embarrassed by what I had said to Neely, even more so, now that she had poured her heart out to me. I hadn't known that her journey had been such a volatile one. "I'm sorry, Neely," I confessed, sheepishly. I remember her wrapping both of her plump arms around me and giving me the warmest hug that you could imagine, then she kissed my forehead.

***

My recollection of Neely's childhood, was abruptly interrupted, as I was snapped back into the present time, by the sound of Neely's voice, "Bliss, I will not be ignored, girl. Stop bein' rude and speak up, would ya?" Neely stood up and marched over to me. I didn't actually see her stand up, as my eyes were still fixed on the carefree dancing bubbles in the sea of the brown Dr. Pepper in my glass, as I had been daydreaming. I knew that she was heading my way by the loud stomp of her feet. I could pick that waddle pattern out anywhere. Then, there they were, her fat ankles popping out of her dingy white Keds tennis shoes. I wondered how long the laces were gonna hold up before they snapped in two, they were stretched so thin, to accommodate her permanently swollen feet. "Girl, you best look at me," she scolded, "you are goin' to college, I'm gonna see to it. I got some money saved up and I'm gonna find some work first thing tomorrow. I did grab the coffee can before our big break, ya know. I ain't stupid. Now if I come up short, we'll take out a student loan or somethin'. We will find a way, darlin', that's the kind of women we are, that's how we do." I smiled at her, with a small tear in the corner of my right eye. I knew once I blinked, it would make its way down my cheek. I decided that I would let it stay there, in my eye, for just a moment longer, until I could pretend to sneeze into my hands and discretely wipe it away. I didn't want Miss Dahlia to think that I was an emotional wreck, she might not let us stay here very long if she thought that I was annoying.

"So, anyways, Dahlia, tell us more about what type of music Mr. Mathias likes to play," Neely changed the subject, on my account, I'm sure. I know that she saw the tear that was about to make its debut on my face. She probably felt like I had done enough crying for one day and she didn't want to test me. I was hungry and emotional. Neely, of all people, knew that those two were a dangerous combination, when it came to me. Dahlia answered, "Well, Mathias plays four instruments, believe it or not. He plays guitar, bass, saxophone, and piano. He is also an amazing singer. That boy has some pipes, yes he does. Mmmmhmmm. I'm tellin' y'all, he could make a grown ass man cry with his singin'. He loves to play jazz. Actually, he is in a jazz band. They play every Friday night during the summer at my place." "They play here?" I puzzled. "No, dahlin'," Dahlia started with a shake of her head and a grin. "I own a little bar and jazz club on Bourbon Street. I also own a little shop right next door to it." *Miss Dahlia is a business owner, how cool,* I thought. It made me look up to her even more. It also explained her 'independent woman' speech she had given me out by the garage, earlier that day. "What kind of shop?" I asked. "Oh you'd love it, Bliss. I'll bring you there tomorrow. We sell spell kits, voodoo and hoodoo supplies, magic charms, items for people's altars, and other oddities. Every Saturday from ten o'clock in the morning until around two or three in the afternoon, I am booked solid for my famous psychic and past life readings. "That sounds amazing!" I exclaimed. "I'm very proud of it," Dahlia commented as she took the last sip of wine from her glass. "Want me to pour you another one?" I offered. "Oh honey, you've had quite the day, you just sit there and chill. I will go get it myself, thank you though, you are such a sweet girl." Dahlia replied. "I really don't mind," I insisted. I wanted to be able to observe Mathias' kitchen skills, plus it would get me a moment alone with him. "Well, if you insist, honey. Yes, I'd love some," Dahlia conceded, as she handed me her wine glass.

I strolled into the kitchen, nonchalantly, and made a beeline for the refrigerator. "Smells divine," I complimented. "Oh, hey, Bliss. I didn't hear you sneak in here," Mathias remarked. "Whatcha makin'?" I inquired. "Red beans and rice with some cornbread," he boasted proudly, with a huge smile on his face, revealing his adorably slightly crooked teeth, that I had already fallen in love with. "Well, well, well…" I started, nudging him, playfully, "stickin' to your New Orleans roots, I see. Do you only cook Cajun style, or do you have other tricks up your sleeve?" "I've got a few," he said, as his light green eyes locked in on mine, and his hand brushed against my bare shoulder, as he reached for the stirring spoon that was resting on the counter behind me. My stomach did a somersault. Our eyes were locked in on eachother, I could feel his energy pulling me in. I wanted to brush the lock of hair away from his forehead. I wanted to lay my head on his shoulder. I wanted to feel his strong arms wrap around my body, arms that would keep me safe forever, arms that would never let harm come my way. I could tell that he felt the energy between us as well. *I have to be the first to look away, I thought. Don't give him the upper hand, play it cool. He has a girlfriend, remember. Don't let him reel you in like this. He's taken. Don't get wrapped up in his stunning good looks,* I told myself. But I couldn't look away. I knew I should. I knew that I needed to, for my own sake. I had to protect my heart from being broken. But I couldn't resist the intensity of his gaze. Our connection was interrupted by the sizzling sound of rice boiling over on the stove. "Oh shit," he exclaimed, as he grabbed the pot handle to move it off of the heat. "I'm sorry, I distracted you," I apologized. "Don't be sorry," Mathias said, as he placed his hand on my shoulder and slowly traced the outline of my arm with his fingertips, "you have nothing to be sorry about," he said as his fingertips reached my wrist, then he took my hand in his and squeezed it gently, before slowly touching my fingertips and letting go.

"Bliss, baby, did you find the wine?" Dahlia's voice cut through the moment, as she entered the kitchen. I quickly turned my attention back to the refrigerator and Mathias turned his to the stove top. "Um yeah, I got it right here, Miss Dahlia," I replied nervously, as I grabbed the bottle out of the fridge door. "Okay, I was just checkin' on ya," she said, with a voice that eluded to the fact that she had seen us holding hands. I uncorked the bottle of pinot grigio and poured her glass with a trembling hand. I couldn't believe the magnitude of attraction that had just occurred between Mathias and myself. My entire body was buzzing. You know the feeling you get when your foot falls asleep, you know, that tingling sensation? I had that feeling encompassing my whole being. I felt electric and I loved it! Once I had returned the unused portion of the wine, back to the fridge, I followed Miss Dahlia back out to the living room, pausing, just once, in the archway that led from the kitchen to the hallway. I glanced over my shoulder, looking first at the crystal mosaic kitchen floor, then I slowly looked up at Mathias, through my long eyelashes, then, without hesitating, I turned and continued my strut into the hallway. *You looked damn good doing that*, I told myself. I had seen that sexy move on many of the television shows that I watched. It was always a favorite go-to of the popular pretty girl in the shows. From my T.V. watching research, it seemed to work to get the guy every time, without fail. I hoped that my research wouldn't steer me wrong.

I visited with Miss Dahlia and Neely for a while longer in the living room, as our hottie chef finished cooking for us. We ate our dinner in the garden, at a table that Miss Dahlia had set up underneath a large live oak tree. It was breathtaking. It was like a scene from a fairytale. Miss Dahlia had twinkle lights wrapped around the trunk of the live oak, along with a gorgeous chandelier hanging from one of the majestic tree's branches. "This is gorgeous," I complemented. "Yeah, Thi and I rigged this up when he was about fifteen or sixteen," Dahlia replied. "Thi?" I asked with a smile, pointing at Mathias, "Thi's him, right?" She laughed, "yes, that's the nickname I gave him as a child, Thi, as in Ma-Thi-as." "Cute!" I admitted. "Yep, mom loves to call me Thi or Bow-Thi," Mathias added with his infamous grin, as he took a swig of his beer. *Damn, that boy is all kinds of handsome,* I thought, as I watched him take a drink. "Supper was delicious, Bow-Thi," Neely commented, teasing Mathias. "Ha ha, well it was my pleasure cooking for the three most beautiful women in the world," he said, as he winked at me, causing me to blush. Suddenly, I was thankful for the cloak of night. The soft lights of the chandelier kept my secret, hiding the crimson splotches, that I was certain were covering my décolletage. "Let's all get inside before these dang mosquitoes eat us alive," Dahlia suggested, as she blew out the candle in the middle of the table, and began clearing the plates.

Once inside, I helped Dahlia with the dishes. Mathias wanted to do them, but we insisted that the chef never does the dishes. After a couple of minutes, he gave up the fight, and retired to his room. "See y'all in the morning," he said, looking directly at me, "Sleep well, ladies." Miss Dahlia walked over to him and kissed him on the cheek, careful not to get the soap suds from the dishwater on his clothes. "Goodnight dahlin'. I love you. May The Creator wrap her arms around you and protect you," she said. "I love you, too, momma. May She wrap her arms around you and protect you, too." There was something incredibly intriguing about their exchange. It was obvious that it was a nightly routine for them. Probably not when he was away at college, but I was sure they said it every time he was back home. They had probably done it for Mathias' entire life. *How lucky he is,* I thought, *to have a mother like her, so open minded and loving.* When Dahlia returned to the sink, I asked her how long they had been saying that to each other. "Sayin' what, baby?" she questioned. "May The Creator wrap her arms around you and protect you," I answered. "It's a unique thing to say, I've never heard it said before. I've never heard anyone refer to The Creator as a female before. I mean, I have always thought that She was a she, but I didn't know that anyone else did. I was a little surprised to hear y'all say that." Miss Dahlia nodded her head, as she continued to wash the dishes, as I dried the clean ones. "You're probably wonderin' how a woman who does healin' and owns a voodoo and hoodoo shop can say that, am I right?" she inquired, looking right at me. I was afraid that I might have offended her. "No, I didn't mean anything like that," I explained, "I know you practice hoodoo, not voodoo. I know that hoodoo practitioners are often religious. Y'all can practice any religion you want, right?" Dahlia nodded, with her eyebrows raised and a closed mouth smile, which told me that I had impressed her with my knowledge. "What are y'all talkin' 'bout?" Neely said loudly from the kitchen table, where she was sitting as we did the dishes. "Good for you, Neely, for teaching Bliss the difference between voodoo and hoodoo," Dahlia praised. "Oh of course," Neely added, "Bliss knows that we don't mess 'round with voodoo, no ma'am. She knows that voodoo is a religion, in and of itself. We are hoodoo women! Hoodoo people can believe in whatever they want to. As for me and Miss Bliss, we are open minded, we believe in higher beings, God, Mother Nature, our spirit guides, angels, Jesus, the whole nine yards. Hell, we both grew up in New Orleans, how could we not be open minded? You are open minded 'bout that stuff too, right Dahlia?" "Yes, ma'am, "Dahlia answered. "I just love, love, love what you and Mathias said to each other just a second ago. Girl, that is just so cute!" Neely gushed.

"Yeah, I've tried to raise my boy right. I try to keep him open minded. We started sayin' that to each other every night when he was only two years old. It started because one day he said to me that God was a woman. Intrigued, I asked him why he thought that. Heck, I thought that it might've been on account of him seein' my Virgin Mary statues or my Marie Laveau pictures or somethin' like that. He was so sweet, he looked up at me with his lil' toddler eyes and said that before he was born, he was in heaven with God and that she was a woman," Dahlia reported. "Well looks like you done good," Neely exclaimed. Once the kitchen was clean and the dishes were put away, Neely and I decided that we should go ahead and get some rest. As we walked down the hallway towards our temporary room, Dahlia walked up behind me, wrapped her thin arms around me and whispered, "Goodnight Bliss. I love you. May The Creator wrap her arms around you and protect you." "I love you, too, Miss Dahlia. Thank you for taking us in. May She wrap her arms around you and protect you, too."

The guest room that Mathias had set up for us was quaint and cozy. I loved it, I felt protected. It was evident that Miss Dahlia rarely had guests stay overnight, as the walls were a stark white and had no pictures hung on them. The room consisted of a queen sized bed, with a white down comforter that looked as soft as a cotton ball. At the foot of the bed, was a folded patchwork quilt that looked familiar to me. As I approached the bed, I confirmed my initial thought, it was! It was my quilt. Neely must have packed it for me. I couldn't wait to get snuggled in the bed and pull the quilt all the way up underneath my chin. I loved the feel of quilts. They always had some weight to them. I craved having the heaviness being draped over my body. It somehow made me feel safe and secure, it was my comfort zone. I also loved that quilts usually had a story to them. Stories of how they were made with love and passed down through generations. I knew that because Neely had told me that her grandmother was the best quilt maker in 'the whole damn state of

Louisiana', back in her day, and that when she passed into her next life, she left Neely three of her most treasured quilts. Neely had given me one of those quilts when I was little. It was that very quilt that was nicely folded, ready to use, lying on the foot of the bed. The quilt was an exquisite array of purple, gold, and green; the colors of Mardi Gras. Neely had told me that her granddaddy had been a member of the Zulu Social Aid and Pleasure Club and that every year, he would ride in the Mardi Gras parade with the Krewe of Zulu. Her granny had made that quilt to represent what Mardi Gras meant to them. I knew that the quilt was special, and I had always taken really good care of it. I knew that it was a big deal that Neely entrusted me with such a precious family heirloom. I was glad that Mathias had laid the quilt out for us.

Chapter Seventeen

The next morning, I woke to the enticing smell of bacon frying. I rolled over and noticed the empty space next to me. *Neely must already be up and at 'em*, I thought, as I slowly sat up, stretched my arms high above my head, leaned side to side, and yawned, all at once. *Yes, I know, I am quite the multi-tasker*, I thought, as I shook my head and giggled. There is just something satisfying about stretching first thing in the morning, it was one of my favorite feelings. I would often stretch my legs as I got dressed. It had become a habit. I loved to challenge my flexibility by putting on my shoes and challenging myself to tie them without bending my knees. I would often watch T.V. while sitting in some sort of contortionist position. I would tell myself, just hold it until the commercial break, come on, you can do it. Years of being a bored homeschooled kid, with no social life had paid off, as I was now as flexible as an Olympic gymnast. Of course, if I had it my way, I would be a prima ballerina, not a gymnast. I had the graceful movements and the long and lean body of a dancer. Neely loved to watch me dance. Of course, my stage had always been my bedroom, and Neely was the only audience member. It made not one bit of difference to me, I danced like I was performing in front of twenty thousand people. Neely would hoot and holler, "Ooh baby girl, get it! Yeah girl, you got some moves," she used to say. She usually caught me imitating the dancing on the music videos that I watched on a daily basis on MTV's show, Total Request Live. I must admit, I was damn good, especially for having no formal dance training. I had always wanted to take dance classes, but of course, my controlling mother wouldn't allow it. Everyone has a natural talent, something that they are good at, something that makes their vibration so loud, that Mother Nature, herself, beams with pride. I knew that dance was my thing.

I remembered being three years old when Neely introduced me to a movie that is still one of my all-time favorites, to this day; The Wizard of Oz. I will never forget that first time that I saw the ballerinas in Munchkin Land. I knew, right then and there, that I wanted to be a dancer. I begged my mother to let me take ballet lessons, when she repeatedly told me no, I turned to Neely for backup. She tried her damndest to persuade Cecily Fontaine to let me take dance class, but Cecily didn't want me to be able to excel in something. Heaven forbid that I learn self-confidence and poise.

I wondered if Dahlia had been a dancer, she certainly looked like one. I hoped that she was. I wanted to be able to show her my self-taught ballet foot and arm positions. I needed them checked for accuracy, as I had only read about them in a book that Neely had checked out for me from the local library. The book was from the 1960s and the pictures were faded, but at least it gave me a general idea of the positions. *Hopefully I will have time to ask Miss Dahlia when she brings me to see her businesses today*, I thought. If my prediction was correct, and Dahlia was a dancer, then she would get about a gazillion cool points, in my book.

I hoped that I hadn't slept in too late, causing Dahlia to leave without me. There wasn't a clock in the guest room, so I had no idea what time it was. I figured that I better follow the bacon aroma to the kitchen and get my day started. As I opened the guest room door, to step out into the hallway, a wonderful thought poured through my mind and hugged my soul. I was no longer tethered, no longer chained. A puppet no more, my free spirit could thrive and blossom into my true self. If I wanted to take dance class, I could. A new chapter had begun, in the life that I was living. Actually, I take that back, a whole new book had begun, not just a chapter. It was up to me to write it. I knew, without a doubt in my mind, that I was going to be the best damn author, of the Book of Bliss, that I could be. My life was going to be lived. I decided, right then and there, that I would take every bit of angst, every bit of suffering, every bit of oppression that had been forced upon me and I would use it. I would morph it into fuel for my dance, my art, fuel for my soul. *Every artist needs inspiration, good or bad, well congratulations momma, all of the neurotic shit you put me through is going to inspire me to be better than you, so I suppose that in a twisted, messed up kind of way, you were my muse.* I came to a realization, in that very moment. I realized that I was the only person who could author my story, no one else could make my decisions for me any longer. I was the writer, composing my life's story, and I was going to make it a good one.

I was in a state of euphoria, high from my realization. Oblivious to the fact that I was dancing down the hallway, doing some of the basic ballet movements that I learned from the old ass library book. *Martha Graham, move over, here comes Bliss Fontaine*, I said to myself, as I pas de bouree'd down the hallway, towards the kitchen. I was snapped out of my trance, when the sound of applause and whistles echoed behind me. I whipped around and saw Mathias peering out of his bedroom door, cheering wildly. I was so happy about my newfound independence, that I didn't even get embarrassed. I laughed and curtsied, then stood up, faking arrogance, and said, "Thank you, thank you, adoring fans. No autographs, please!" Mathias laughed and disappeared back into his bedroom. I skipped into the kitchen, smiling like a tick that had found herself a fat dog. "Well goodmornin' sleepin' beauty," Neely said from the kitchen table, where she was drinking, what was probably her third cup of chicory coffee. "Mornin'," I replied. Miss Dahlia was standing at the stove, fryin' up the bacon that had lured me from my slumber, she turned around and commented, "Well someone is awfully chipper this mornin', did ya sleep well, Bliss?" I took a seat next to Neely at the kitchen table, grabbed her coffee cup and took a swig. "Yes ma'am," I answered, as I set the coffee cup back down. "You make a mean cup of coffee, Miss Dahlia," I complimented, "I think that's the best coffee that I've ever had the privilege to taste." Neely looked at me and stuck her tongue out, playfully. "Oh Neely, you know I grew up on your coffee, and it is amazing. I mean, it made me the addict that I am today, I wouldn't be a caffeine junkie, were it not for your coffee, but you gotta admit, this is some next level stuff right here," I continued, "I mean, your coffee is like some top of the line marijuana, but Miss Dahlia's coffee is like angel dust. No offense, I'm just sayin'." "It is some good shit," Neely replied, as she snatched her cup back from me, while donning her famous alligator smile. "Well thank you, sweetheart, but I can't rightly take the credit for this coffee. You can thank Café Du Monde for that nectar of the gods," she said as she grinned and gestured towards the can of coffee grounds that read, 'Café Du Monde Original French Market Coffee Stand, Coffee and Chicory'. "Get ya some, girl," she suggested, as she gestured towards some empty coffee cups that she had placed near the coffee pot. "Don't mind if I do," I said, with a shimmy. "Woah, someone's gettin' fancy this mornin'," Dahlia commented. Hearing that from Miss Dahlia, about myself, was one of the best compliments that I could think of, considering that Miss Dahlia was most definitely the prettiest and fanciest person that I knew. She was fancy in a classic type of way. Not in a, 'hey everyone, look at me, look how rich and fake I am', type of way. Miss Dahlia was just a naturally graceful and beautiful person. She exuded femininity and mystery. I hoped that I could be like her someday.

"Miss Dahlia, random question, but were you a dancer?" I blurted out, as I poured myself some of that dark brown, roasted goodness. "Well, that is a bit of a random question, dahlin', but I like random, and yes, I was a dancer. I grew up taking ballet and jazz lessons, and I actually majored in dance in college. In fact, I am still somewhat involved in dance, as I am the choreographer for the stage shows at my nightclub." Dahlia answered, as she put the last piece of fried bacon onto the plate, and turned the stove burner off. "Y'all hungry?" she asked, as she set the plate of bacon and a plate stacked with pancakes down in the center of the kitchen table. "Yes ma'am," I replied, feeling the saliva moisten the corners of my mouth. When food smelled incredibly good, my mouth became the Colorado River, with the Hoover Dam knocked down. As I sat down at the kitchen table, with my cup of greatness, I swallowed my spit before speaking. "So, Miss Dahlia, do you do the hiring of the dancers for your stage shows?" I inquired. "Well I'm the queen bee up in there, so you betcha I do," she replied, with a laugh. I took a sip of my coffee and reminded myself that no woman ever got anywhere without taking a leap of faith and putting herself out there. Miss Dahlia brought over a plate of biscuits and a bowl of white gravy. "Y'all dig in," she insisted. I swallowed my saliva down once again, as Dahlia took a seat at the table with us. I had to swallow, partly because the food smelled so damn good, but also because I was about to put myself out there and I was fearful that Miss Dahlia might shoot me down. *Write your own story*, I told myself. "Um, Miss Dahlia," I began timidly, "Hang on one sec, sugar," she said hastily, as she held her pointer finger up at me and craned her neck towards the archway that led to the hallway. "Thi! Breakfast is ready, son!" she hollered. "Okay Bliss, go ahead now honey," she encouraged. "Well, I was just wondering, I mean, if it isn't any trouble, or a big deal," I began, "I'll be there in a minute, mom!" Mathias' voice echoed down the hallway, interrupting me, mid-sentence. Dahlia put her pointer finger up to me again, signaling me to hold on for a minute. "Mathias, it's gonna get cold, now c'mon!" Dahlia yelled. I waited to see if he was going to respond to his mother's commands, attempting to avoid being interrupted during such an important conversation. It could possibly be a life changing conversation, I thought, as I took a deep breath, preparing to begin again. "So anyways, Bliss, I'm sorry that I stopped you, I just hate for people's food to get cold, then it ain't no good anymore," Dahlia advised. "You got that right," Neely agreed, with a mouthful of biscuits and gravy. I looked at Neely and some of the white gravy was dripping slowly down her chin. *Gross*, I thought, as I became increasingly more annoyed that I couldn't finish my question. I snatched Neely's napkin from underneath her butter knife and

handed it to her abruptly. "Wipe your chin, Neely," I insisted.
"Okay, somebody's got her panties in a wad," Neely replied, her
eyes wide, looking at Dahlia across the table. They both laughed.
"Where is that damn boy?" Dahlia inquired, her irritability growing
by the second. "Mathias!" she screamed. Dang it, was I ever going
to get to finish my question without getting interrupted? We heard
footsteps thudding down the hall, getting louder as they approached.
"Here he comes," Dahlia said, with a satisfied grin on her face.
Mathias stuck his head around the corner, looked right at his mom,
and pointed at the cellular phone that was attached to his left ear.
Dahlia motioned for him to come over and sit down. Mathias,
obviously frustrated, mouthed, "I'm on the phone". Dahlia shook her
head as Mathias turned quickly and stomped back towards his room.

"I swear, that boy gets his temper from his father," Dahlia
commented. "Sorry y'all had to see him act like a butt head," she
apologized. "No harm done," Neely said with a shoulder shrug. I
don't think Dahlia even heard Neely. She had a look on her face that
eluded to the fact that the wheels in her mind were a'turnin',and she
was about to get lit up. "I mean, really? Like he can't call her basic
ass back after breakfast? What the hell is that? Rude. That's what it
is. Ugh, I swear, that girl gets a kick out of having him wrapped
around her finger. I'm sure she just loves it that he told me no and
continued to talk to her ass. She knows I don't like her. She's not
right for him, I can feel it. I am not a hateful person, but I do not see
what Thi sees in her. She's basic. She has no originality, nothing
interesting about her whatsoever, and she's entitled. I mean, entitled
as hell, you know that type of girl, that acts like she's not happy
unless she has the latest designer purse and designer jeans?" I
nodded my head in agreement and added, "Oh yes, I've seen those
type of girls on T.V. shows. It's so stupid! It's like their entire self
esteem is dependent upon what they have, not what they know, or
who they are as a person."

Dahlia stood up and walked to the pantry, nodding her head emphatically, as she grabbed the syrup off of the shelf and brought it back to the kitchen table. "Exactly! You get it, Bliss. I'm so glad you get it!" she said as she patted my hand. "Oh, I get it!" I said, with wide eyes, imitating Miss Dahlia's emphatic head nod. "Sounds like that girlfriend of his is just a basic bitch," Neely exclaimed, with a mouthful of bacon. I handed her napkin to her, once again, and we all busted out laughing. We must have laughed for a good two or three minutes. We laughed so hard that tears were streaming down our faces and Neely had to get up from the table to make a beeline for the bathroom, before she peed in her panties. As she rounded the corner we heard her say, "Oh hey, Bow-Thi!" That made Dahlia and I laugh even harder. I was wiping tears from my eyes as Mathias made his way into the kitchen, looking grumpy as hell. He didn't say a word, he just sat down at the far end of the table and dished himself up some food. "Nice of you to join us," Dahlia prodded. "Whatever, mom," Mathias replied, with a frown. I took a long sip of my coffee and used my trick to keep myself from busting out laughing again. I knew that Mathias was in a mood and I didn't want to set him off. I was picturing the starving children from the charity commercial, when Miss Dahlia broke the silence. "So, anyways, Bliss, you never did get to finish what you were trying to tell me earlier." I swallowed and started, "Oh yeah, well I was wondering if I could maybe audition to be a dancer in your stage shows." Before Dahlia could reply, Mathias let out a chuckle. I whipped my head in his direction, narrowing my eyes, in an attempt to tell him to shut up. I looked back at Dahlia and continued," I mean, I don't have any formal dance training, but it has always been my passion. I'm a fast learner, too. I would practice for hours a day, until I get the choreography just right. If you would just give me a chance, Miss Dahlia, that's all I'm asking for. I just need someone to give me a chance." I barely got the last word out when Mathias started laughing again. I turned toward him, scowling, and said, "What the hell is your problem?" He didn't answer me, he just continued laughing. I decided to ignore him, as I turned my attention to Dahlia. She was looking at Mathias, with a look that said, 'you better compose yourself right now, or else'. He stopped laughing, and mumbled that he was sorry. Then Dahlia turned her attention back to me and said, "Bliss, I think that you would be a lovely addition to my show. You are a beautiful young lady, and I can sense that you would be dedicated to the choreography. I do need to tell you though, that my show is not ballet. I mean, don't get me wrong, I love ballet, but let's be honest, people who come into my bar on Bourbon Street are not looking to see a rendition of Swan Lake." "That's alright, I've studied up on jazz dance and I can perform any of the hip hop dances from any of the TRL music videos that have aired since '98. I mean, that's a solid two years of videos, and I have most of the dances memorized. Whatever it is, Dahlia, I can do it, just give me a chance." I pleaded. "Alright, dahlin', I'll give you a chance," Dahlia said, as she stood and brought her plate and coffee cup to the sink, "I'm gonna go get changed into some dance clothes. I will lay a leotard and high heels out on the bed in the guest room. Meet me in the living room in ten minutes, to learn your audition choreography." "High heels?" I asked. "How am I gonna do pirouettes in high heels? Can I just dance barefoot for the audition?" I inquired. Dahlia was in the archway, ready to step into the hallway, when she turned around, smiled, and replied, "No honey, it must be high heels. The show you are auditioning for is a burlesque show." With that, she turned and walked out of sight.

I looked at Mathias. "Now you know why I was laughing," he said. "I seriously cannot picture you as a burlesque dancer," he teased. "Why the hell not?" I asked, angrily. I didn't even know what burlesque was, but as long as it was something to do with dance, I was all for it. It pissed me off that Mathias doubted my skills. "You just have this goody-goody type of look. I mean, don't get me wrong, you are beautiful, naturally beautiful, which is a rare thing nowadays. I just can't picture you acting sexy, that's all," he confessed. "If that's supposed to be a compliment, you really suck at it," I lashed out. "I can be sexy," I insisted, "I am sexy, you'll see." I stood up and brought my dishes to the sink. As I walked toward the archway, I turned back and confessed, "Now I just have to figure out what burlesque is." Just as I said it, Neely returned from the powder room. "Who be talkin' 'bout burlesque?" she asked, as she plopped down into the chair that she occupied minutes earlier, and shoved another piece of bacon into her mouth. "I am," I said, "Miss Dahlia choreographs a burlesque show at her nightclub and I am going to audition to be a dancer in it." I looked right at Mathias and nodded matter-of-factly. "You go girl!" Neely said, as she gave me a high five. "Hang on there a second, girl. How do ya know what burlesque is, anyhow?" she asked. "I don't," I admitted. "Ooh, girl, you so pretty, you'll be great." She assured. Then she turned and looked at Mathias, as she continued, "This girl here can dance, boy, I'll tell ya. She's gonna have every guy on Bourbon Street droolin' over her." Mathias looked at me and I shrugged my shoulders. "Well I better go get ready for my audition," I said. I turned to leave and glanced over my left shoulder as I rounded the corner. Mathias was staring right at me, and if I didn't know any better, I would've thought that Neely's statement had uncovered a tinge of jealousy in him. *He doesn't want guys looking at me*, I thought, with a pleased expression on my face, as I made my way to the guest room, to put on my audition outfit and begin writing the first chapter of the book of my new life.

Chapter Eighteen

Two days had passed since Dahlia had taught me the choreography that I was to perform for my audition. It was a sexy jazz style routine, choreographed to the song "American Woman", by the Guess Who, not the remake done by Lenny Kravitz, that had come out the summer before. Miss Dahlia told me that she preferred the original version. I surprised myself at how quickly I caught on to the movements. Miss Dahlia told me that I was a natural, but that she wanted me to practice for the remainder of the week and that she would bring me to her nightclub on Friday evening, so that I could have a proper audition in front of an audience. The day had come, and I was ecstatic. I had been wishing for an opportunity to dance on a stage for the majority of my life, this was my moment. "Bliss, dahlin', go on in my closet and pick you out a costume for tonight," Dahlia had suggested, that afternoon. I loved Miss Dahlia's bedroom. I had gotten to see it on Wednesday when she was teaching me the routine.

***

We had started in the living room, but Miss Dahlia had suggested that we move into her bedroom, when Mathias decided to find every opportunity that he could to walk through our rehearsal space, interrupting. I was too busy concentrating, trying to take in each and every detail about the movements, to realize what he was doing. "And, five, six, dig seven, pop eight, roll one, two, up three, ball change, drag five, hip six, shimmy seven, eight….Mathias! We are trying to concentrate, stop that!" Dahlia had scolded. I turned around, and there Mathias was, making a fool out of himself, imitating every movement that I was doing. I had turned back around towards Dahlia, rolled my eyes, and grinned. I couldn't stay annoyed with Mathias, he looked too damn cute, imitating the hip rolls and shimmys. Miss Dahlia was not amused. After the third warning, she was over it. "Come on Bliss, let's finish this up in my bedroom, where we won't be disturbed by immature twenty year olds," she insisted, as she yanked the boombox plug out of the socket, gave Mathias a look of disapproval, and stormed off, through the archway, disappearing into the hallway. "Alright then," I said as I turned to follow her. As I turned to glance back at my imitator, I was surprised to see that he was right behind me. He placed his hand on my shoulder, which sent chills down my arm, smiled at me and said, "Hey Bliss, you know I was just kidding earlier in the kitchen, right? I didn't mean to piss you off or anything. I was just givin' ya a hard time. You're gonna be great." I grinned and replied with a soft, "Thank you." As I turned to leave, he gently grabbed my forearm and continued, "You're a gorgeous dancer, and um, yeah well, I was stupid to say that I couldn't picture you being sexy. You *are*." Embarrassed, Mathias cleared his throat, and hurriedly left the room. I was stunned, my heart was pounding, and for a moment, I swear, I stood as still as the Persephone statue at my mother's house. I wanted to imbed every detail of that moment into my memory forever. The way his hand felt on my skin, the deep tone of his voice, the sound of his breath, the way he licked his lips before he spoke, the adorable way that he shifted his weight nervously as he said, "you *are*." I loved everything about that moment. I was beckoned out of my temporary statue form, when Miss Dahlia's voice echoed down the hallway, "Bliss, come on girl, we gotta get this eight count down before you can take a break." "Coming!" I informed. It had taken us another two and a half hours for me to finish learning the rest of the choreography. Actually, it was probably about an hour and a half of actual dancing and an hour of Miss Dahlia and I chit chatting during my water breaks and her pinot grigio breaks.

I was the instigator of the gab fest when I told her how much I loved her bedroom. Every piece of her furniture looked fancy and glamorous. From her four post, princess canopy bed, draped with black silk, to her oval mirrored vanity, that was adorned with vintage perfume bottles, and her purple velvet chaise lounge. On one wall of her bedroom, Miss Dahlia had three tables pushed together, as her altar. I could have stood and looked at the altar for hours, just taking it all in. She had tarot cards laid out across the table, crystals, gemstones, candles in at least five different colors, a statue of the Virgin Mary, a crucifix, rosary beads, a scrying mirror, a crystal ball, numerous bottles of oils and potions, a picture of Marie Laveau, a spellbook, flowers, shells, coins, a cow skull, and an alligator head. Next to her fancy bed was a small nightstand, which had an ornate frame sitting atop it. As I sipped my water, during our first break, I inched closer to get a look at the picture. Miss Dahlia noticed that it had captured my attention, and walked towards the nightstand. "Good lookin' guy," I commented, when I got close enough to see the photograph. It was a black and white picture of a handsome man with light hair and light eyes, holding a guitar. "Yep, he sho was, and he knew it too," she replied with a laugh. "That's Mathias' father, back when we was datin'. That was almost twenty one years ago. Time flies, I'll tell ya, it seems like just yesterday. I knew that it was not polite to pry into other people's lives, but Dahlia had a way about her that made you feel like you could, so I did. "Were y'all ever married?" I asked. Dahlia sighed and replied, "Well that's a long story, sweet girl, but it's quite the cautionary tale, so I think it might be a good one for a young pretty thing like you to hear." She sat down on the end of the bed and patted the comforter next to her, gesturing for me to join her. My body began tingling, as I could sense that this story was going to be rather interesting. Without hesitation, I walked over and sat in the exact spot that she had patted.

***

"Well," she began, "it all started when I was a mere twenty two years old and I had just finished my junior year of college. We were out on summer break and I landed myself a job as a cocktail waitress at a jazz club, not far from where my club is now. I was working one late afternoon when the band that was going to play at the club for the weekend, showed up to get ready for their first set. That mighty fine lookin' guy right there," she said as she pointed at the framed photograph, "was the lead singer and guitarist for the band. That day, he walked his fine ass right up to me as I was wipin' down a table. I will never forget it, I had my back to him and when he started talkin' my stomach got the butterflies. There was somethin' 'bout his voice, smooth as hell. I guess my tummy could tell he was gonna be a looker, just by the sound of him. He had asked me if there was a green room for the band. I turned around and first thing that caught me was those light green eyes of his. Oooh child, I knew right then and there that I was gonna fall for that man. See that's where Mathias got his pretty green eyes from," she said as she nudged me and smiled.

"Oh, Mathias has green eyes?" I asked, trying to make her believe that I had not noticed. I forgot that Dahlia could read people, hell that's one of the things that she did for a living. She knew that I was falling for Mathias, but she was kind enough to let it go, with a simple nod and a response, "Okay, I thought you had noticed, but I guess I was mistaken. Yes, my baby boy has the same light green eyes as Vince did." "Vince was his name?" I inquired, trying to get the focus off of Mathias' eye color, as I could feel that I was already blushing. "Mmmhmm," Dahlia confirmed with a grin. "Yep, so anyways, I introduced myself to him and his band and showed them back to the green room. I ended up talkin' to my manager and I offered to work a double shift that day, just so I could watch Vince perform. Silly, I know, but I was smitten as hell. Well, he ended up being in town for two months, playin' different gigs with the band that summer. Those were some hot and heavy two months let me tell ya. Oooh girl, we was head over heels in love with eachother. We just had a connection, like we was meant to be, or so I thought at the time. Vince was from Ohio and since the band had only planned to be in New Orleans for part of the summer, he was gonna have to go back to Ohio at the beginning of August. I was so in love with that man that I was ready to quit college, right before my senior year, and leave New Orleans, to go live with him in Ohio. Can you imagine? Oh Lord, it makes me shudder to even think that I was 'bout to leave my amazin' hometown. I'm tellin' ya, Bliss, my spirit guides were workin' overtime that summer because what if I had gone with him to live in Ohio? My life would be completely different. I would have been stuck up there." I wrinkled my forehead and asked, "Well what happened that made you not move there with him?" Dahlia shook her head and took a deep breath, I looked at her face and could see tears welling up in her beautiful almond shaped eyes. *This still hurts her, whatever it is,* I thought. *After all of these years, it still gets to her.* It surprised me to see Dahlia get emotional over a man. She came across as such a strong woman.

My thought was interrupted as Dahlia answered, "You won't believe it. He had moved back to Ohio at the beginning of August and I was goin' to get all of my stuff ready and move two weeks later, in mid August. I missed him so much during the two weeks that he was gone. We had daily phone calls and I wrote him the sweetest love letter and mailed it to him. I couldn't wait to be in that man's arms again. As slow as those two weeks seemed to pass, the day finally came. It was movin' day for me and I was as giddy as could be. The plan was that he was going to fly in, rent a truck and drive to the little college apartment that I lived in, to load up all of my stuff. Then we were gonna drive our asses to Ohio. So there I was, sittin' on my living room couch, just waitin'. His flight was supposed to get in at eleven in the mornin', which would put him at my place around noon or so, after he rented the truck and what not. Well noon rolled around and Vince wasn't there, I still waited patiently. Twelve thirty comes and he's still not there. I told myself that planes are sometimes delayed and that it was no biggie. Once one o'clock came 'round, I kinda started gettin' worried, and I had a bad feelin' come over me. I wasn't as confident in my psychic abilities back then.

Listenin' to my intuition could've saved me a lot of heartache, but I'm glad that I didn't know what was about to happen, as I never would've had anything to do with Vince, which would have meant that I wouldn't have my Mathias. So anyways, I'm gettin' on a tangent, sorry. I know you're anxious to find out what happened.

Well I had that bad feeling come over me, I just knew somethin' was up. I called the airline and that flight had landed on time, at eleven o'clock that morning. Now remember, Bliss, this was before car phones or cellular phones, so I had no way to get in touch with him, if he was on the road. So I decided that I'd go outside and sit on the front steps and wait for him, that way, I could see him turn onto the street, which would give me an extra forty seconds or so of seeing my man." With that, she laughed and shook her head, "Yep, that's how crazy I was 'bout him. So, I go outside and wait awhile, no sign of Vince. The only car that drove up was the mailman. I stood up and went up to retrieve my mail from him, I knew it was all going to be junk mail, but I figured that it would give me somethin' to do while I waited. I thanked the mailman and went to sit back on the step as I sifted through the envelopes. There was a thick one, addressed to me, written in big bubbly handwriting, that I didn't recognize. The postmark was from Dayton, Ohio. I quickly opened the envelope and pulled out a thick, folded letter. It was at least ten pages thick. As I unfolded the letter, a photograph fell out and dropped to the ground. I bent over to retrieve it, and I immediately went hysterical once my eyes focused on the image. There he was, Vince, in all his handsome glory, wearing a sharp lookin' tux, standin' next to a beautiful bride. I turned the photo over and through my tears, I could barely make out the handwritten bubbly letters, 'Vince and Marissa June 1977'.

I hurried into my apartment, afraid of what the neighbors would think, were they to see me losin' it over a damn picture. Of course, all of my neighbors were college students, as the apartment complex that I lived in was student housing, and most of the students were back in their hometowns for the summer, but I didn't want to chance bein' labeled as a crazy girl. That's just social suicide, right there. Ya know what I'm sayin'?" I nodded emphatically, "Yes, I know exactly what you're sayin'," I replied. Dahlia continued, "I mean, I knew I wasn't crazy, but it just seems like people, well guys mostly, but some bitchy girls too, are so quick to call a girl crazy, when she is not. It's sad really, it's like young girls feel like they aren't allowed to be sad or upset, or even stand up for themselves, for fear that they might be labeled as a crazy ass girl, and no one wants to be that. Guys are expected to get upset, angry, yell, and hell even hit things when somethin' bad happens to them, but we are taught from a young age that 'girls don't yell, young ladies don't get angry', I always hated that. My momma force fed that mentality to me ever since I could talk. My momma would tell me that young ladies, when angered, should shove their hateful feelings down into their push up bras and make their boobs look bigger. Now that shit is crazy! It's like saying, 'hey you, yes you, impressionable young lady, don't have an opinion on things, just make your boobs look bigger and life will be glorious'. Well I say, to hell with that!" Dahlia looked at me, patted my knee and sighed.

***

"Oh look at me, goin' off on a tangent again. Sorry, Bliss, it's just that I'm not used to havin' a strong young lady 'round here. I like it. Oh and you're so sweet, lettin' me vent. Anyways, we can get back to the choreography now, dahlin'," she said as she stood up. I gently touched her shoulder, "I'm enjoyin' our conversation, just a few more minutes, please, Miss Dahlia? I don't mean to be nosy, but I wanna know what that dang letter said. Did you ever read it?" I inquired with a sheepish smile. I knew that the letter had most likely either made her incredibly forlorn, or it had pissed her off to no end. I wasn't quite sure if it was appropriate to smile about it, although it had been twenty one years, some wounds never heal, and I certainly didn't want to offend this beautiful woman who was exposing one of her darkest moments to me.

***

"Well hell yeah, I read it, you best believe it!" Dahlia declared proudly. "It was a long ass letter from his wife, Marissa, tellin' me 'bout how long they'd been together, that they were high school sweethearts, and stuff. She told me that he didn't know that she was sendin' me the letter or the picture, but that, woman to woman, she felt like I deserved to know the truth about Vince. She said that she had checked the mail one day and found the love letter that I had sent to him. She apologized for reading it, but said that she had a feelin' that he was goin' behind her back again. Apparently she had caught him cheating with three other women, in different cities that he had gigs in. The letter went on and on, I don't remember all of it. I think I blocked parts of it out of my memory, because it was just too damn painful to think about. I mean, Vince really treated me like I was special. Like I was the love of his life, and all along he had a wife waitin' for him at home. Poor Marissa, having a dead beat, poor excuse for a husband, like him. You know Vince finally called me two days later and said somethin' about gettin' tied up in a gig in Los Angeles and that he was so sorry that he couldn't make it back to New Orleans. He said that if I would give him until December, he could come back and get me.

I didn't tell him about the letter. The man that I thought I knew, was an illusion. If Vince had no problem lying to me, his wife, and at least three other women, then I wasn't sure what he might be capable of doin', and a dog backed into a corner can be vicious. I didn't want to put Marissa in danger, or myself, for that matter. I just told him that I needed to stay and finish school and that once I graduated, I would get in touch with him the next summer. I was lying right through my teeth, but I had to. Quite frankly, I was scared of what he might do.

I found out, the very next day, that I was pregnant with Mathias. I was overjoyed! I cried tears of joy, when I saw the results of the pregnancy test. I knew that I didn't need Vince. I was going to raise my baby on my own and do a damn good job, at it." I put my arm around her shoulder, hugged her and confirmed, "You did. Mathias is a great guy." She looked at me, kissed my cheek, and replied, "Thank you, baby girl. I know he can be a butt head sometimes, like all boys can, but I know for a fact that he would never be hateful to a woman, he would never be verbally or physically abusive to a woman, and I know he would never cheat on a woman." I felt the heat rise up my neck and cover my face, I was sure my skin had turned from porcelain to crimson.

***

The shift was caused by Miss Dahlia's last statement. The one when she said that she knew that Mathias would never cheat on a woman. I felt a tinge of shame in my gut. *I shouldn't be upset by her statement. It's a good thing for a man to be faithful.* I hated that I was jealous of his girlfriend, Jennifer. Ugh, I couldn't even stand to think of her name. I felt the acid rise up in my throat and I quickly swallowed it back down. It tasted disgusting, but I had no choice. Regurgitating my biscuits and gravy would make Miss Dahlia think one of three things, none of them were good. She would either think that the gravy had turned, that I couldn't handle the dance rehearsal, or she might think the truth, that I had a thing for her son and that I was jealous of his girlfriend, whom I'd never even met. None of those scenarios would shine a positive light on me, so I decided that in order to save face, I needed to change the subject, and fast.

"Well, I've taken up enough of your time, Miss Dahlia. What do you say we go over the routine one more time, and then I can rehearse on my own and give you a little break?" I suggested. "Sounds good, thanks for givin' me someone to vent to. I just wanna say one mo' thing, before we go back to dancin'. I want to make sure that one thing is clear," she said, in a tone that made it obvious that she meant business. My stomach flip flopped, as I took a deep breath, and said, "Okay." I just knew that she was going to probably scold me about my jealousy, but she didn't. Instead, she gestured towards the framed photograph of Vince, and said, "I know that you are probably wonderin' why the hell I would have a framed picture of that man next to my bed, after all of these years." I was quick to interrupt her. "Oh no, I wasn't wondering that at all, Miss Dahlia. What you do, is your business. I have no right to question your decisions, I know that."

Miss Dahlia leaned in towards me and continued, "I just want you to know that I don't usually have his picture displayed like this. I actually got it out a few days ago, 'cause I was gonna burn it durin' a spell that I wanted to try. It's a spell to shield me and Mathias from his negative energy forever. I just haven't had time to do it yet, with everything that's gone on. I don't long for him or miss him, nothin' like that. I know I made the right decision to raise my baby boy by my lonesome. I'm glad that I did that. Mathias wouldn't have turned out the way that he has, had I made a different decision, a selfish decision. I am proud of myself for putting my unborn child's needs before my own. Sure, I was a heartbroken mess for a good long while. My family disowned me when they found out that I was expectin' and unwed. Actually, they didn't disown me right away, they tried to marry me off to my momma's friend, Miss Mary Lou's son, Samuel. He was a student at Tulane with me. I had met him at my parent's parties and what not. He was a nice guy, I mean I had nothin' against him. I just thought that it was a twisted idea. Momma just wanted me to marry him because he was in school to be a doctor, plus his parents were wealthy, and I think she also wanted me to marry him because he was white, and my unborn baby was gonna be half black and half white. I know it sounds crazy and messed up, but my momma was all about how things looked to other people. She cared too much about how society would think of her. I hated that about her. I guess that's why I have always tried to live my life the opposite of that. I live my life to be authentic to myself, not to please other people. If people don't approve of my choices, well to hell with them!" she said with a dramatic wave of her hand and a laugh. "I know exactly what you mean, Dahlia. That's how my mother is, too. I don't ever want to be like that," I agreed.

Dahlia placed her warm hand on my arm and gently squeezed it, as if to tell me, 'thank you for getting me', then she continued, "My momma had found this here picture of Vince and so she knew that he was a white guy, I knew that was the main reason she had her hopes set on Samuel and I gettin' hitched, so that everything would look 'normal'," she said while doing air quotes and rolling her beautiful eyes. "I swear, my momma and Mary Lou had their hearts set on gettin' what they wanted. My daddy just went along with it. He was always that way, whatever momma wanted, momma got. So, of course, when I told momma that I was dead set on finishin' school, gettin' my degree, and raisin' my baby on my own, she got in a tizzy. I just knew daddy was gonna come a'knockin', and he sure did, but I'm gettin' a little ahead of myself. Let me back it up a bit. I started the fall semester at Tulane, my belly growin' by the week. When December rolled around, I was full on showin' and there were plenty of busy bodies who made it quite obvious that they were lookin' at my ring finger on my left hand for a weddin' ring. When they saw that it was bare, they'd whisper to their busy body friends, if none were around, they'd settle for givin' me a dirty look. Oh, I probably got about twenty dirty looks a day, but I didn't give a single damn. I was independent and happy. Well, my momma kept on keepin' on 'bout tryin' to get me to marry Samuel. Miss Mary Lou even offered to buy us a house and a brand new car if we got married. She kept tellin' me that the baby and me would be taken care of and that I could live a life of leisure, being a doctor's wife. I told her that bein' somebody's wife and nothin' else just wasn't good enough for me. I was gonna be somebody. That is somethin' that I want you to remember, Bliss. Just bein' some guy's wife should never be enough for you. It isn't! You've got so much greatness ahead of you, baby girl, I can see it!" I smiled as I wiped away a tear that had begun to make its journey down the side of my nose. "Thank you, Dahlia," I whispered. "I mean it, girl. Bein' in love and marryin' a man is wonderful, it's a beautiful thing. I don't want you to think that I'm all anti-man or against the union of two souls. That ain't it at all. Yes, I am a feminist, but I still love men, hell I raised one. People get all creeped out by the term feminist. It doesn't mean that I'm a man hater or that I don't want to wear a bra or shave my legs. Hell, I love lookin' pretty, and that's okay. I'll be the first one to say, that's part of the reason that I own two businesses and a home and have gotten this far is because of my looks. My smarts played a big role as well, don't get it twisted. I'm just sayin' that you should rock what ya got!

***

Anyways, back to the story, when momma saw that I was bound and determined to do things my way, she turned to desperate measures. She had my daddy cut me off completely. They stopped payin' for my college. They disenrolled me, without tellin' me. I showed up at class one day and the professor gave me the news in front of the entire class. I was mortified! Then, I return to the parking lot to find my car missing. They had taken it. I walked to the bus stop and took a bus back to my apartment. When I arrived there, I found my parents loading up the last box of my belongings. I was beyond upset. I felt like my freewill was being stripped from me. I couldn't understand why my parents wouldn't want me to succeed on my own. Why weren't they on Team Dahlia? They should be proud that I wanted to finish school and make somethin' of myself. But no, it wasn't how they wanted things to play out, so they wouldn't allow it. I didn't know what to do. I had nowhere to go, not a penny to my name. I felt like I had no choice but to get into my dad's car and go to live with them, so I did. I needed time to figure out what to do next. I lived with them until Mathias was two months old. I couldn't stand to live in such a judgmental household that allowed no personal freedom. I bolted on the day that was to be my weddin' day."

As Dahlia said that, my ears perked up, "Your wedding day? To Samuel?" I asked. Dahlia looked at the ground and nodded slowly, she took a ragged breath, looked up and began fanning her face with her hands, in an attempt to dry the tears that were falling down her face. "Yep, my momma and Miss Mary Lou were not goin' to give up on that. Nobody outside of my family knows any of this, Bliss. I just feel like you get me. I don't know everything about what ya went through with yo' momma and daddy, but I do know tid bits that Neely told me. Plus, my third eye shows me pictures of some of the madness that went on in yo' house. I know that you felt like a caged animal. You always knew that you had so much to offer the world, big things ahead of ya. You know that you're special, you're not average in any way. I felt the same way about myself. I know that our circumstances were quite different, but I think they both evoked the same type of emotion within our spirits. The feeling of being trapped and wantin' nothin' more than to bust out of the box that you've been contained in. Just wantin' to bust out with your bright aura just castin' light beams all over the whole damn place!"

***

My heart was pounding fast. She knew exactly how I had felt. We were kindred spirits. "Yes, that's it, exactly," I confirmed. "Bliss, I want to tell ya that I have had visions of you since before you were born. My spirit guides told me that they had connected with your spirit guides long ago. We have helped each other in our past lives, we are linked together. Everything that I experienced during my childhood and throughout my young adulthood, with my parents, was necessary for me to experience, so that I could help you. My guides wanted for me to be able to understand how it felt to grow up in an oppressive household, to feel caged, longing for things to be different, to crave breaking free from the people who live to hold you back. I didn't have as intense of a childhood, as you had, but I felt every pain that you felt, as you were feeling it. I also escaped from my momma, 'cept I had a two month old baby with me. "What did you do?" I inquired.

***

"Well, momma didn't want Mathias to be at the ceremony. Guess she was afraid of what her uppity friends would think. Hell, she had hid the fact that I had been pregnant and had a baby from everyone that they knew, except for Samuel and his parents. Her crazy ass plan was that we were gonna get married and act like I got pregnant on our wedding night. Then she would just tell everyone that I was on bed rest, doctor's orders, during my pregnancy, and that I couldn't have visitors. She had planned that, for seven months after our wedding day, I would be basically quarantined in the new house that Miss Mary Lou and her husband had bought for us. Then they would act like I had gone into labor early and had the baby pre-maturely. She was so damn crazy! Remind you of anyone you know?" she asked. "Yes it does, that is a Cecily Fontaine move, if I've ever heard one!" I exclaimed with a shake of my head.

Dahlia continued, "So, they had already planned that my aunt was gonna babysit Mathias at the house that she worked at, on the day of our weddin'. My aunt was my daddy's sister and momma wanted any excuse not to invite her to the weddin'. She didn't care for her at all. Momma was afraid that my aunt might embarrass her, or some shit, at the weddin', so she put her on babysittin' duty. I had only met my aunt like maybe two times in my life. Momma didn't like her comin' 'round. I just acted like I was goin' along with everything. I knew that I was goin' to escape, I had to. I was not gonna let my life be dictated for me. Plus, I knew, that you were gonna be born two years later, and that I had to get out of there, in order to be ready to help you."

***

I looked at her, my eyes wide with wonder and amazement, "You knew about me, even then?" I asked. "Yes, baby. I've always had my gift of being able to predict things, Although they were not always as practiced and strong as they are now. I was able to talk to my spirit guides, and Shenequa has shown me things for as long as I can remember. I didn't know how to recognize synchronicities as easily, back then, but I did have the gift." she answered. "Shenequa?" I puzzled. Dahlia started laughing her ass off. She could barely catch her breath, but when she did, she patted me on the knee and answered, "Yes, baby, Shenequa is a silly nickname that I gave my third eye. I forgot that I hadn't told ya that!" We both laughed.

I loved how cool Miss Dahlia was. It made sense that we were kindred spirits, I loved everything about her. She was an open book. She had nothing to hide. She had an air about her, an air of conviction. She had lived and had no regrets. She was compulsively unapologetic about the choices that she had made. She looked at every obstacle in her path as an opportunity, never as a hindrance. Mistakes that she had made were not given the chance to set her back, no. She took every stumble and turned it into a leap. She transformed every negative experience into an opportunity to grow, an opportunity to overcome. I could just sense that about her. She was a strong woman, the kind of woman that I hoped that I could be.

"I've gotta know, Miss Dahlia, what happened on the day of your big break?" I inquired as my foot that dangled off of the bed shook quickly from side to side. I couldn't sit still, my scalp felt like it was on fire and I wanted to dance on the ceiling. The story was getting good and juicy. I was hanging in suspense, barely able to stand it any longer, when we heard a knock on Dahlia's bedroom door. "Yeah, come on in," Dahlia invited. The door opened halfway and Neely peeked her head in. "Am I interruptin' y'all's rehearsal?" she asked. "Just a minute, Neely, Dahlia was tellin' me somethin' important," I stammered. *Damn, why did she have to knock right then, right when Miss Dahlia was about to get to the good part,* I wondered. "No, no, it's fine, come on in, Neely. I was just about to tell Bliss about the day that I made my great escape and became an independent woman with a capital 'I'," Dahlia said with a grin. "Oh, yeah, this is good, it's real good. Bliss you gonna really like this part baby," she said as she looked at Dahlia and winked. "You already know?" I asked, as I looked at Neely, "But, I thought…" "Just listen, Bliss," Dahlia insisted, gently, as she continued.

***

"Well, I packed up Mathias' diaper bag and I threw a few of my valuables in there as well. I couldn't take much, because I didn't want my momma to get all suspicious. I did manage to put some stuff in the zip up garment bag that held my weddin' dress. I grabbed a quilt that my great great grandmomma had made, oh it was so precious to me because it had been passed down from my great grandmomma, to my grandmomma, to my daddy, then to me. She was the best quilt maker in all of Louisiana, I tell ya!"

***

As Dahlia made that claim, I nudged Neely with my elbow and grinned. Neely had claimed that her great grandmother was the best quilt maker in the state. I knew that it must've been eating Neely up inside, hearing Dahlia say that. Neely just looked at me and grinned, then turned her attention back to Dahlia's story. Dahlia kept right on talking.

***

"I slept with it every night. It was a comfort thing for me, so I put that in the garment bag. I ended up shovin' my expensive designer weddin' dress behind the toilet. I wasn't gonna be needin' it! My momma had left to go to the beauty shop to get her hair done for the weddin' and daddy had grabbed the newspaper and headed to the bathroom. I knew that was my chance! I called the house that my aunt worked at and asked her to come pick me and Mathias up. I had found her phone number scribbled in my momma's address book, earlier that week. I didn't dare take the address book, or write it down, for fear that my momma would figure my plan out. I memorized that phone number like my life depended on it, which it did. I had called my aunt late one night, earlier that week, and told her my plan. She was all in. She understood how crazy my mom was, and how my daddy just went along with anything my momma said."

***

Dahlia paused, as she grabbed her wine glass and took a nice long sip of her pinot grigio. My foot began to shake anxiously again, as I was eager for her to continue the story. She set her glass down on the nightstand, and commenced her recollection.

***

"The house that she worked at was in the same neighborhood as my momma and daddy's, so it only took her a couple of minutes to get to us. I knew that my daddy would be indisposed for a good twenty five minutes, at least. His bathroom routine was like clockwork. I gathered the rest of the things that could fit into my aunt's car, while she held Mathias. As I ran outside with the last bag, my aunt told me to hurry up, as she pointed back at the house behind me. I remember lookin' back and seein' my daddy lookin' at me from his bedroom window. He didn't look mad. He looked proud. I think he was proud that I had the guts to leave. That I wasn't going to end up wasting my life, being miserably married to a man that I didn't love. He waved at my aunt, his sister. Then he blew a kiss at me, and I swear I saw tears in his eyes. I got into the passenger's seat, Mathias sitting on my lap, and I held Mathias' tiny little hand up and did a little wave to his grandpa as we drove away. That was the last time that I saw my daddy."

***

Miss Dahlia paused as she reached for a tissue from the box next to her bed. She wiped her eyes and sniffled, then she grabbed another tissue and handed it to Neely. *Neely probably has a booger hanging out of her nose,* I thought, as I turned to look at her. I was wrong, she didn't have a dangler. Neely was crying. I mean, tears flowing down without an end in sight, kind of crying. *Neely has known Dahlia for a long time, she probably feels connected to her too, causing her current downpour of emotions,* I reasoned to myself. Neely had never told me how they met, but I knew that they had known each other since before the night that I killed my father. Neely had brought me to Miss Dahlia's house that night, she had known exactly where to bring me. I was only four years old back then, so I knew that they had met sometime before then. *Thank God that Neely met Miss Dahlia,* I thought. *Where would we be right now without her?*

Both Dahlia and Neely took a few minutes to regain their composure. Once they did, Dahlia continued.

***

"So, my aunt brought me and Thi to the house that she worked at. We stayed there for four or five weeks, hidin' out from the wrath of my momma and Miss Mary Lou. I just knew that they had probably been madder than wet hens and embarrassed as all get out, when they discovered that I was a runaway bride. My aunt's employers were a young couple, with no children yet. They were off, vacationing in Fiji, so my aunt, myself, and Mathias had the entire house to ourselves. I was so grateful for those weeks, and for my aunt. I truly do not know where I would've gone, had it not been for her."

***

I put my arm around Dahlia, hugged her, and laid my head on her shoulder, as I softly said, "Your aunt sounds like an amazing woman. I would love to meet her someday." Miss Dahlia gingerly placed her long fingers underneath my head and lifted it slowly off of her shoulder, turning it slightly in Neely's direction. "You already have." Neely said, with her alligator smile.

Chapter Nineteen

We arrived at Miss Dahlia's nightclub as the sun goddess, Hathor, was taking her last bow of the day, allowing Selene, the moon goddess, to make her debut. As we stepped into the dimly lit club, the smell of booze and cigarette smoke filled the air. It was only eight something in the evening, but the place was packed already. Miss Dahlia led the way through the crowd of party animals, stopping every few seconds to hug someone that she knew and to say hello to familiar faces. I followed closely behind her, trying my damndest not to get lost in the sea of tipsy patrons. A jazz band was up on the stage, performing like their lives depended on it. The club was loud, humid, dark, crowded, and chaotic, in all the best ways. I loved it! I couldn't wait to get on the stage and dance my little heart out. I had never been to a place like that before. Hell, I'd hardly been to any public places in all my seventeen and a half years. The only parties that I had witnessed were my mother's hoity toity brunches, which were always prim and proper, and had Emily Post written all over them. It would be a stretch to call the brunches parties. There was absolutely no fun to be had at them, whatsoever. I would consider them gatherings, not parties. Miss Dahlia's nightclub, on the other hand, was most definitely a party, in every sense of the word. It screamed New Orleans. Every aspect of the club paid great homage to my favorite city in the entire world. The energy was palpable. The atmosphere was electrifying. I was enthralled by the scene, trying to take it all in. I must've ran smack dab into Dahlia, at least five or six times, as we made our way to the door that led backstage. Every time that Dahlia would stop to greet someone that she knew, I was inevitably looking in another direction, taking in the people and the ambience. Thank goodness Miss Dahlia was patient with me. She didn't once cast me a disapproving look. Neely, on the other hand, had the misfortune of walking behind me, which meant that every time that I ran into Dahlia, Neely ran into me, and Mathias ran into Neely. "Pay attention, girl. Damn!" Neely demanded, irritated as hell. "Sorry 'bout that, Neely, I'm just trying to take it all in," I explained. "I know that, girl, but every time you ain't payin' attention, I run right into ya, which makes Bow Thi over here run into my ass. He's steppin' on the back of my Keds, makin' them all dirty and shit. I knew I shouldn't have gotten the darn white ones!" she exclaimed, as she turned and looked at Mathias, giving him the stink eye. "Neely, those damn Keds have seen better days," I informed, with a grin, as I winked at Mathias.

We eventually reached our destination, the big red door which led to the backstage area. "Knock 'em dead, girl," Neely encouraged, as she gave me a thumbs up with her left hand. Her right arm was still bruised and sore. Dahlia had hooked Neely up with a makeshift sling, made from the stuff that you would use to wrap up a sprained ankle. "Be careful with your arm," I told Neely, "don't let anyone bump into it." "Yes mom," Neely joked. I turned toward Mathias and said, "Watch her, will you? Make sure no one bumps into her." "Aye, aye, captain," Mathias said with a sarcastic salute. I smiled, shook my head, and followed Miss Dahlia through the exclusive red door.

The backstage area was dusty and cluttered, but I loved it. I was born to be a performer, I could feel it deep inside of me. This was it. I belonged here. My invisible ant friends returned to their familiar location on my face and scalp, causing a tingling sensation to spread throughout my entire being. Instead of being overcome with a feeling of dread, the ants provided me with a feeling of excitement. I preferred for them to bring the positivity, although I had to give them props for being my watchdogs, always warning me of impending danger. Right then and there, I knew that the imaginary ants, were my cheerleaders, rooting for me to put on an amazing performance.

Miss Dahlia showed me to a dressing room. It was a tiny room. The walls were painted black. There was a small costume rack on one wall, and a vanity with a mirror framed with giant light bulbs on the back wall. A small, velvet tufted ottoman sat in front of the vanity, acting as the chair. I hung up the costume that I had chosen from Miss Dahlia's closet, and proceeded to touch up my makeup. Once I was dolled up and ready to perform, I emerged from the dressing room and informed Dahlia. She gave the music to the sound technician, held up her pointer finger, as if to tell me to hold on a minute, as she ascended the three steps, that led up to the stage, and disappeared through the curtain. Seconds later, I heard her voice on the microphone. "Listen up, all you pretty people! You are in for one hell of a treat. Takin' the stage for her burlesque debut, is Miss Lily Dahlin'!" A roar of applause, hoots, hollers, and whistles, filled the air. "Go ahead, Miss Dahlin'," the sound guy urged. I turned, looked at him and pointed to myself with a puzzled look, as I asked, "Me?" He nodded and gestured towards the stage. "Yoo hoo, Lily Dahlin', yo' audience awaits," Dahlia said, as I climbed the three steps and made my way through the velvet curtain, onto the stage that would either be a catalyst for my aspirations, or a catastrophic fail. I've always been a 'glass half full' kind of gal, myself, so I chose to think of the stage as a catalyst.

I could barely make out the audience as I made my way to centre stage. The spotlight shone brightly on the silver sequined costume that I had snagged from Miss Dahlia's closet earlier that afternoon. I felt my vibration intensify. I felt alive. This was where I belonged. I took my beginning position, for the "American Woman" routine. Dahlia winked at me as she held her microphone and said, "There she is ladies and gents. Le bon temps rouler!" With that, she left the stage and my music began. I'll say it. I danced the shit out of that routine. I was right on with every movement. The crowd loved it! When I hit my ending position and the audience applauded, I was on cloud nine. My eyes had somewhat adjusted to the spotlight, allowing me to make out Neely's plump body in the sea of drunk asses. She couldn't clap, on account of her arm being in a sling, but that woman was beaming. She had her full on alligator smile. I knew that she was proud of me. My eyes shifted to the right, where Mathias stood, with two fingers from his right hand in his mouth, whistling with all his might. I was flying. Soaring through the sky on adrenaline, when the wind got knocked out of me. I saw her. Standing next to Mathias, his left arm around her shoulder, looking boring out of her mind. *That must be Jennifer,* I thought, *she must have gotten here when I was in the dressing room.* My moment of jealousy was interrupted when Miss Dahlia's voice rang out through the crowd once again. "Fabulous job, Lily! Isn't she hot, guys?" Cat calls and applause echoed throughout the venue. I flashed a sly smile and made my way off of the stage, and into the wings.

As I entered my dressing room, the thought struck me, that I would have to meet Jennifer that night. It was inevitable, there was no avoiding it. I wasn't sure if I could manage being fake nice to her. I hated having to act fake nice, although I had become a master at it. Yes indeed, I had honed the craft of fake nice during my mother's social gatherings. *Why did he have to invite her on my big night?* I wondered. I began to take off the sequined dress, when I heard a knock on the dressing room door. "Um, just a minute!" I said. "Bliss, it's just me, Dahlia, can I come in?" she asked. "Sure," I responded. She opened the door no more than a foot, turned sideways and shuffled in, closing the door behind her. I proceeded to change from my costume, into my normal clothes. Dahlia clasped her hands together, did a little bounce and squealed. "You were fantastic, baby! Everyone loves ya! I knew they would. Oh, and how did ya like yo' stage name, huh? Pretty clever, isn't it? Yep, I came up with that one all by my pretty little self," she mused. I snickered and admitted that I appreciated the stage name. "It has a great ring to it," I stated. "Well, most of the other performers don't have a stage name, they just use their real names, but I figured we better use one for you, since you never know if word might get 'round to yo' momma, that a beautiful girl named Bliss be breakin' hearts and takin' names at Ten

Sheets," she commented. "What's Ten Sheets?" I inquired. "Ten Sheets. Like Ten Sheets to the Wind," Dahlia answered. I shrugged my shoulders, still puzzled. I didn't know what she meant by that. Surprised, she tried further explanation, "You ain't never heard that sayin' before? Well usually people will say three sheets to the wind, talkin' 'bout somebody who's drunk off their ass, but I wanted to go further with it, so I named this place Ten Sheets. You didn't notice the sign on the outside of the buildin' when we got here?" "I guess I was too focused on everything else. Cool name, though!" I replied.

I had finished my metamorphosis, from Lily back to Bliss, and was hanging the costume on the clothing rack when there was another knock on the door. Dahlia went over and opened it. It was Neely, Mathias, and the girlfriend. "Hey y'all!" Dahlia exclaimed, "Did y'all come to visit the next big star?" "Ya betcha!" Neely said, in her loud and proud voice. I walked over and wrapped my arms around Neely. "Can you believe that I am a real dancer now?" I asked. "I always knew that you would be," Neely said as she squeezed me tightly. I turned to grab my makeup bag, as Dahlia said, "Thi, aren't you gonna introduce Bliss?" Mathias cleared his throat, looking uncomfortable, as he mumbled, "Oh yeah, um Bliss, this is Jennifer, Jennifer, that's Bliss." Jennifer looked at me with a bitchy look that said, 'just so you know, I am intimidated by you, but I'm gonna pretend that I'm not impressed by you one bit. I'm gonna act nice in front of my boyfriend so that he won't realize what a bitch I am, but I will only put forth the minimum amount of effort into my act. My boyfriend, although smart and handsome as hell, is like all guys, naturally oblivious to tension between members of the opposite sex. I know that it will drive you crazy for me to act this way because, girl to girl, you can sense the truth. You will also have to put up a fake ass front, so that my boyfriend won't peg you as the mean girl, as I can tell that you want to stay in his good graces, in hopes that he will fall madly in love with you and dump my ass. So yes, I will shake your hand right now. I will tell you, through gritted teeth, that you performed well on the stage, although I can't stand the fact that my boyfriend was mesmerized by your every move. I will smile the universal smile that every girl knows is code for, I hate your guts. I will be polite out of obligation, nothing more.' I extended my hand, she obliged, and we shook hands, as I mumbled, "Nice to meet you." "You too," Jennifer replied, as she narrowed her plain ass, dookie brown eyes. "We need to celebrate," Dahlia exclaimed, "How 'bout we all go out for a late supper?" Neely perked up, "Yes, ma'am, I am one starvin' marvin! I'm definitely down for some grub." With that, we left the club, went to a casual restaurant down the street, and had the most awkward dinner that I could imagine.

Chapter Twenty

I worked at the nightclub for the next several weeks. I loved performing on the stage, being in the spotlight. It was my comfort zone. I no longer got nervous before performances, just excited. I was at home on the stage. I had also taken Neely and Miss Dahlia's suggestion about attending college. I submitted a late admission application to Tulane University. I had already been accepted to LSU, but Baton Rouge was an hour and a half away, and I didn't have extra money to pay for a dorm room or an apartment. Miss Dahlia suggested that I apply to Tulane, her alma mater, so that I could live at the house with her and Neely, while I went to school. Thank goodness, I am one hell of a writer, if I do say so myself. I wrote an amazing essay, that I submitted with my application for enrollment. My essay brought to light, feminist thought regarding the Greek mythological figure of Medusa in literary history. I talked about how Medusa is a symbol of female rage. According to Ovid, the famous poet who wrote Metamorphoses, Medusa was once a beautiful virgin. However, after being defiled in Athena's temple, Medusa was punished by Athena. Her punishment was Athena transforming Medusa into the startling figure, with snakes for hair, that we all recognize from popular mythology. Ovid's opinion was that Medusa got what she deserved. My essay was written from the opposite position. I disagreed with Ovid. I wrote from a feminist perspective, highlighting the fact that women need to stop hurting other women. We have enough opposition and oppression from men. As women, we should be advocates for each other, we should be allies. We are on the same team, we seem to forget that. I talked about the importance of eliminating the patriarchy, which, unfortunately, still exists in our everyday lives. My essay shed light on the double standard that, unfortunately, exists in our modern day society. The fact that many people view guys who have promiscuous sex or who have even date raped a girl, as acting the way that they expect guys in our generation to act. I have seen numerous movies and TV shows use some variation of the phrase, 'boys will be boys', or 'that's a guy for ya', however, if a female is promiscuous, she is called a 'slut', or worse. It is a double standard and it is completely unfair.

I was proud of my essay. It had opened doors for me. Not only the door to attending Tulane, and obtaining a higher education, but a door to bettering myself, as well. I realized that I was hating on Mathias' girlfriend Jennifer. I had hated on her before I had even met her. Sure, she had been rude to me the night that we met, and every time that I had seen her since, but I made the decision to steer clear of the , oh so tempting path of jealousy. I would take the high road. I didn't need to be pining away after Mathias anyhow. I had big things brewing, and I wasn't going to let a guy slow me up.

Contrary to what you might assume, the inspiration for my essay was not the Mathias and Jennifer situation. My inspiration happened during my third week as a burlesque dancer at Miss Dahlia's nightclub, Ten Sheets.

***

It was a Saturday night and I was performing. I noticed a handsome guy sitting on a barstool watching me from stage right. He was gorgeous, so gorgeous that my attention seemed to gravitate towards him every few eight counts. I was mesmerized. He had me hook, line, and sinker, and I had not even met him yet. Let this be a cautionary tale, girls. Do not fall for a guy just because he is a hottie. A guy needs to have substance, he needs to be respectful, he needs to get you. Good looks don't hurt, but make sure that his good looks aren't masking his issues. Afterall, appearances are fleeting. Our physical appearance just happens to be the body that we were given to experience this time and place with. We are not our bodies. We are not our looks. We are spiritual beings, put into a body in order to have a human experience. We have each had numerous human experiences, we just cannot remember them. We are dealt situations in order to learn a lesson. A situation will continue to arise, until we figure out how to overcome it, and learn from it. That is the meaning of life, constantly learning and bettering our souls. I wasn't about to let my stupid jealousy of a girl that I barely knew, hold up my enlightenment, so I decided to let go of my envy and just do me.

Back to that Saturday night, I had finished my last set of dancing. Now, let me make this clear, during my burlesque routines, I was fully clothed. I never took my top off, never wore pasties, nothing like that. My costume was a black corset, fishnet tights, and black lycra dance shorts, with black knee high boots. It was no more revealing than what the New Orleans Saints' cheerleaders wear. Some burlesque dancers reveal almost everything they've got on stage. Now, I'm not staying that I have anything against that. I am all about basic human rights and people having the freedom to choose what they do and how they live their life. My philosophy is, hey, it's their body, their decision, it's just not my thing. Now, I want to make this very clear. I am not explaining my costume, in order to get approval from you, or anyone else, for that matter. No offense, I was still trying to find myself, back then. I had not yet embraced the unapologetic attitude that I now have. I was still a teenager, for goodness sake. I wasn't as self-assured as I am now. I had gumption, and plenty of it, I just wasn't quite sure if it was appropriate for me to use it on a regular basis. Now cut my teenage self some slack, yes I was still seeking approval from people in some ways, but I think a lot of that was because I had never been allowed to have friends and socialize in a normal fashion. I wasn't allowed to have attention. I think that is part of the reason that I loved the stage and the spotlight so much, and why I craved companionship, I knew that I didn't need it, I just wanted it. I have since developed the philosophy that I do not need validation or approval from anyone, except for myself. I wish that I had lived that philosophy back then, but hell, life is a learning process, and boy, have I learned.

Anyways, I was finished with my last set and I was headed to my dressing room to change into the denim skirt and sparkly top that I had worn to the club, before heading home. Side note, it was nice to be able to call Dahlia's house my home. She insisted on it. Being able to have such a wonderful and loving home made everything right with my soul. As I was walking back to my dressing room, I was thinking about going home, and curling up with a good book in the hammock that hung in the garden, when my thoughts were interrupted by Damian, one of the club's bouncers, as he said, "Hey, there's a guy that wants to meet you. I can tell him to get lost if you want me to." I turned my gaze in the direction that Damian was pointing, to assess if the guy looked like a perv or not. To my surprise, it was the guy from stage right. The dreamy guy. My skin felt flushed as I nervously replied, "Oh, uh, no, that's okay, Damian. I'll go talk for a sec." I made my way over to the hunk and extended my right hand to shake his, "Hey, I'm Lily," I said. He grinned, took my hand and instead of shaking it, he kissed it. "Pleased to meet you, I'm Jake," he responded, with an accent that was unmistakably New Orleans. I felt kind of silly introducing myself, using my stage name, but Dahlia had insisted that I use the name Lily whenever I was at the club. She said that Lily would lose some of her allure if I didn't stay in character. "Miss Lily, would you care to join me for a drink?" Jake asked. Of course, I knew that I wouldn't be able to order a drink, being two weeks shy of eighteen, so I responded, "Well, I really don't like to drink where I work, but thanks for asking." He offered to bring me to another bar on Bourbon Street. I wondered how I was going to get out of revealing my age to him. Technically, I shouldn't be allowed to even be in the bar, being under eighteen and all. I didn't want to get Miss Dahlia or anyone else in trouble, so I knew that I had to keep up my mature façade. "I'm pretty exhausted, I think I better just go on home. I'd love to see you at another show, though," I hinted. Jake, not willing to give up, suggested that we grab a bottle of wine and some cheese from a nearby store, and that we head over to New Orleans City Park to enjoy some stargazing together. Unable to resist his charm, I agreed. I hurried to my dressing room, changed my clothes, and we were off.

After obtaining our wine and cheese, we arrived at the park. Not many people were there, just a few couples that were enjoying each other's company. Jake found us a nice park bench that was secluded with massive oak trees surrounding it. We sat down, and he proceeded to open the wine bottle with a corkscrew that he had thought to purchase at the store as well. Part of me had secretly wished that he had forgotten to buy a corkscrew, which would make us unable to open the wine bottle, which would mean that I would not have to drink. I didn't have anything against drinking. It was just somewhat scary to me, as I had never had wine or any adult beverage, before that night. Sure, I had taken one sip of Mathias' beer, but I had never actually drank before. I was afraid that I might look foolish, or do something that would make it obvious that I was an alcohol virgin. I was not only an alcohol virgin, but I was an actual virgin, as well. Hell, I had never even kissed a guy before. I didn't know the first thing about kissing. As handsome as Jake was, I was hoping that he wouldn't make a move, out of fear of the unknown. Jake looked to be at least four or five years older than me, and I was willing to bet that he hadn't been as sheltered as I had. The thought that he was probably very experienced scared me. Don't get me wrong, I longed to be kissed by a guy. *Jake would be a great first kiss*, I thought. He was handsome and charming, and he had nice full lips that I was sure would be soft and comforting, were they to meet mine.

We sat and talked, sipping on our wine and savoring the gourmet cheeses that he had purchased. He looked like he probably came from a wealthy family. He was dressed nicely, and he spoke eloquently. He had that rich guy look. You know, the one, where they have perfect white teeth, perfectly combed hair, good skin, dressed like they walked out of a Ralph Lauren magazine ad. Also, his black BMW, didn't hurt my assumption. He said that he was from New Orleans, but that he was going to be a senior at Darmouth University. He had come home for the summer because he said that there was nothing to do in New Hampshire. "Don't get me wrong, I love Darmouth, but living in Hanover, New Hampshire for nine months out of the year, can really put a damper on a guy's social life. Especially if that guy is born and raised in New Orleans, the best city in the world," Jake boasted.

I agreed with him on the whole, New Orleans being the best city in the world, thing. There was no place that I'd rather live. I wanted to live in New Orleans for the rest of this life, and all of my lives to come. I just hoped that the city was big enough to keep me out of sight from my mother. I never wanted to see her again. I was pleasantly startled back to the moment at hand, when Jake put his arm around me and pulled me closer to him.

"Look at how big these oak trees are," he said, looking up above us, "It's crazy to think that these oak trees have been here for hundreds of years, and they will be here long after we are gone from this life. Just think of all that these trees have seen. If they could talk, I'll bet you that they could tell us some good stories." "Yep," I replied. I knew that I should have elaborated. I wanted to elaborate, but I was still taking in the fact that this gorgeous guy had put his arm around me. I was on cloud nine. He seemed perfect. "Yep? That's it? Just yep?" he asked, in a lighthearted teasing tone. I blushed as I looked at him. "Yep, just yep," I said, as I shrugged my shoulders and smiled. We both laughed and our eyes met. He gently put his hand on my cheek and drew my face close to his, as he pressed his lips against mine. My heart was pounding, and the familiar butterflies made their presence known in my stomach, as we continued to kiss. We kissed for a long time. I couldn't stop, he was addictive. As our kisses intensified, I wanted the night to last forever. He gently lifted my body and put me on his lap, guiding my legs to straddle his lap, as we continued kissing each other. I was in a daze, mesmerized by him. I didn't realize what was going on, when suddenly I felt him pulling my panties to the side. "No, no, I don't want to do that," I whispered, as I pushed his hand away, gently. We continued kissing for a few minutes when he tried it again. "Please don't," I said, as I pushed his hand away more forcefully. "Come on," he said, as he tried again. I pushed him away, and started to get off of his lap, when he grabbed my hips and forced me to sit where he wanted me to, "Let me go," I screamed as he forced himself upon me, stealing something from me, that I could never get back, stripping me of all of my dignity. I struggled to get away, but he After a few minutes, I broke free from his grasp and ran. I didn't know where I was going, I just knew that I had to get away from the guy who had taken my innocence. As I ran to the edge of the park, toward the street, I heard Jake yell at me from the park bench, "You're such a dirty bitch!"

Tears streamed down my face as I ran. I didn't know which direction to go. Jake had driven us to the park and I had been talking to him as he drove. I didn't pay attention to the direction that he went. The park was about three or four miles from Ten Sheets, I guessed, considering the amount of time that it had taken us to drive there. I knew that three or four miles would be pretty far to run, especially in a skirt and high heels. I came to a street, where I saw, a hole in the wall chicken and waffles restaurant. Out of breath, I went inside and asked if I could borrow the phone. The woman behind the counter reminded me a little bit of Neely, she had the same look. I silently thanked my spirit guides for putting her in my path, I knew that it was their way of lending me a bit of comfort in my time of need.

"Sho' honey, just come on back here and you can use it. It's a local call, right?" she asked. I nodded, "Yes, ma'am," as I struggled to catch my breath. "Everything okay, honey?" Neely's clone asked, with a worried look on her face. "It will be," I assured, as I grabbed the phone and dialed the phone number for Miss Dahlia's house. I was glad that I had memorized it. Our nightly routine was that Miss Dahlia would bring me to the club, hang out for awhile, make her rounds, then she would go back to her house. When I was ready for her to come pick me up, I would call her from the phone in her office. Miss Dahlia had caller ID, so I hoped that she would answer her phone, not recognizing this phone number that I was calling from. It rang five times, then went to the answering machine. I waited for the beep, then said, "Hey, if y'all are there and can hear me, this is Bliss. I'm callin' y'all from a restaurant," I cupped my hand over the reciver and whispered to Neely's twin, "What's the name of this place?" "Mo's," she answered. "I'm at Mo's," I said into the receiver. I was about to ask the lady what the address was, when I heard Mathias' voice on the other end of the line. "Bliss? What's goin' on? Why are you not at the club?" he asked. "It's a long story, but I need your mom to come pick me up. I'm in a bit of trouble, there's this guy.." "I'm coming right now." Mathias stated. "Okay, the address is.." "I know where Mo's is," he interrupted. "Tell the lady behind the counter, that you know me and that I'm on my way. That's Mo'nique, she'll take good care of you. I'll be there soon, just stay put." He said, then hung up.

I returned the receiver to the base and turned around. "Are you Mo'nique?" I asked Neely's twinkie. "Sho' am," she answered. "Well Mathias wanted me to tell you that he's the one that's coming to pick me up," I explained. Mo'nique didn't hesitate, she grabbed a to-go box and started stuffing it with waffles and fried chicken. When she had filled it to its capacity, she handed it to me and reached around me to grab a Styrofoam cup, a lid, and a straw. "Here ya go, sweet girl, just pick a table, put yo' food down, and get yo'self a drink from the soda fountain over yonder," she insisted, "I'm gonna pack up some boxes fo' Mathias and Dahlia too. Y'all can take them with ya." "Thank you so much," I replied, as I chose a table that was hidden by a partition. I wasn't sure how angry Jake was, and I didn't want to chance him driving by and seeing me through the window.

 I attempted to eat, as I nervously awaited Mathias' arrival. I was still shaking and although my crying had subsided, quite a bit, I still had tears rolling down my red cheeks. Food just doesn't taste good, when you're crying. As a child, I had spent many dinners at the dining room table with my bitch of a mother, crying as she belittled me. I hated trying to eat while sobbing. I had always felt like it was unfair to Neely. She worked so hard cooking for me and momma day in and day out for years. I didn't like it when my mother's hateful words ruined perfectly good food. This was the case now. Mo's fried chicken smelled mouth watering good, from what I could smell, through the snot that had accumulated in my nostrils, thanks to a guy who had not been taught hoiw to respect a woman.

I still couldn't believe it, my virginity had been taken, in the most heinous way possible, rape. *I should've never left the club with him,* I thought. *Maybe if I had worn pants instead of a short skirt, this wouldn't have happened.* I knew better than to blame myself. I knew that I wasn't asking to be raped by what I was wearing. *I don't care how a woman is or isn't dressed, she can be stark ass naked, for all I care, if she says "no" or "stop", then your horny ass better stop.* As I replayed the previous fifteen minutes or so in my mind, I went from feeling like a victim, to feeling angry. It wasn't fair! I wanted my first time to be special, with a guy that I was in love with. Jake had taken something precious from me, that I could never get back. *How could he?* My thoughts were interrupted when a hand touched my shoulder, I jumped.

"Woah, Bliss, what's wrong?" Mathias asked, looking concerned. He stooped down to my level and began gently wiping away my tears. I started crying harder. I couldn't speak, I just hugged him and sobbed into his shoulder. Between sobs, I heard Mathias ask Mo'nique if she had any idea what had happened. "I have no clue," she started, "poor baby just ran in here 'bout fifteen minutes ago, cryin' and lookin' scared shitless. She just asked me if she could use the phone to make a call. I have no idea what happened to her before she come bustin' in here. Who is she, anyhow?" Mathias stood up and gently helped me to my feet. "She's livin' at mom's house," Mathias replied, "she works at the club. She worked tonight, I don't know how she got over here from the club." I took a deep breath and cut in, "I met a guy at the club tonight. He was charming and wanted to take me on a date. I just wanted to go on a date," I said, as my voice became almost unrecognizable, as I attempted to stifle my sobs. Mathias reached his strong arm out and pulled me close to him. "What happened, then, baby?" Mo'nique asked. I sniffed, attempting to keep my nose from becoming a snot faucet. "Well, I went with him to get some wine and cheese from the store, then we went to the park. Everything was going great, until he, um, until he…" my voice cracked and I cupped my hand over my mouth, trying to muffle the sound of a loud sob, as I began crying again. "Did he hurt you?" Mathias said in a tone that I had never heard him use before. He was livid. I nodded my head and replied, "He didn't hit me or anything, he um, he raped me."

As I said the word out loud, I bursted into tears again. I was grateful that it was late and that Mo's was empty. I would have hated to make a scene in front of her customers. I looked at Mathias. Even through my tears, I could see the vein in his neck protruding, his fist was balled up, and his jaw tightened. He was angry. Mo'nique walked over to me and gave me a hug, wiping away my tears. "I am so sorry honey, that is horrible. Do you need to go to the hospital?" she asked. I shook my head, "I'm okay, I just want to go home and rest," I said. "Get her home, Mathias, and you call me in the mornin' and tell me how this girl is doin', won't ya?" Mo'nique insisted. Mathias didn't speak, he just nodded and led me out the door and to his car. As he was opening the passenger side door to let me in, a black BMW pulled up next to us.

Jake had his window rolled down, and he yelled, "Hey slut, guess you're gonna go give it up to him now, huh? Bro, let me just tell you, she's not any good, she's not worth it." The next few minutes were a blur, they happened so quickly. Mathias ran over and pulled Jake out of his car, then started beating the crap out of him. I was screaming for Mathias to stop, Jake was in a bad way. Blood was everywhere and he wasn't moving. Mathias seemed to not hear me, he was seeing red. I ran inside of Mo's and told her to call an ambulance. Jake was an asshole, but even an asshole doesn't deserve to get beaten to death. As I ran back out to the street, I heard police sirens and saw a police car speed around the corner. *Someone must have called the cops*, I thought. I had watched enough movies and TV shows to know that Mathias was going to get arrested for sure, and that's exactly what happened.

I begged and pleaded with the police officers. I explained what had happened. I didn't want Mathias to get in trouble over me. I begged until my voice was hoarse, but to no avail. The ambulance came and rushed Jake to the emergency room. New Orleans' finest, read Mathias his rights. I stood on the sidewalk and watched as the police car drove away with Mathias in handcuffs in the backseat.

Chapter Twenty-One

My butt went numb as I sat on the cold, hard bench in the lobby of the police station. Miss Dahlia was talking with the police officer that was sitting at the front desk, whom I was certain, was thanking his lucky stars, at the moment that he had a thick sheet of bullet proof glass in between him and Dahlia. She was a force to be reckoned with. I don't blame her, I was extremely upset by Mathias' arrest as well, but I knew that raising cane, wasn't going to get him out of there any faster. Neely had her arm around me and was squeezing my shoulder, lending me comfort.

***

Once Mathias had been hauled off in the squad car, Mo'nique had called Dahlia. Neely and Miss Dahlia showed up at the restaurant, no more than ten minutes later. She must've been haulin' ass, because it had taken Mathias a good fifteen minutes to get to Mo's earlier that night. The ride to the police station was full of questions. I told Neely and Dahlia the whole story. Both of them were ranting and raving about how messed up it was, the whole, me getting raped thing, and how Mathias was just trying to defend my honor. They didn't think that he should've been arrested. The more they carried on, the worse I felt. I knew in my heart of hearts that none of it was my fault, but I couldn't help but to silently beat myself up inside. If only I hadn't let Jake charm me into leaving Ten Sheets with him, none of it would've happened.

***

"Ma'am, I will let you know more, when I know more, that's all I can do," the officer behind the glass said to Dahlia. "What the hell does that mean?" Dahlia asked. "Is that boy going to be charged with rape? He'd better be!" she yelled. "Ma'am, please calm down, an officer will speak with the young lady in just a moment. The young lady already admitted that she only knew the alleged rapist's first name. I am waiting on the police officer at the hospital to tell me the boy's name, so that we can have that on record when we take her statement. Now, if you'll just have a seat," the officer pleaded. Dahlia obliged, but she couldn't resist letting out one last huff, before turning and taking a seat on the other side of me. "I swear..," she mumbled.

She patted my leg, with a reassuring smile, and added. "It's gonna be okay, baby." I knew that she was saying it more for herself, to calm her nerves. A few minutes went by, when the door next to the window buzzed, then clicked, as it opened and a young female officer emerged. She had sandy blonde hair that was swept back into a low chignon bun. Her skin was the type of skin that looked perfect without a hint of foundation or powder. "Hey there, I'm Officer Dubois. Are you ready to come tell me what happened?" I swallowed the lump that had formed in my throat. I had already had to relive the traumatic rape scene when I told Neely and Dahlia, I wasn't sure if I could do it again, but I knew that I needed to, for Mathias' sake. "Yes ma'am," I responded, as I stood up from my chair and followed her through the door. It felt odd calling her ma'am, as she couldn't have been more than five or six years older than me, but I figured that it was the appropriate response, her being an officer of the law and all. She led me into a room that was secluded from the hustle bustle of the station. She probably wanted me to feel comfortable enough to spill my guts.

I recounted every detail that I could remember from that evening. Good thing she had plenty of tissues, as it was impossible for me to hold back my tears. It felt like a horror movie that was set on a loop, replaying over and over in my mind, toying with me, threatening to drive me insane. I took a deep breath, trying to keep my cool, as I relayed the part of the story that landed Jake in the emergency room. I hoped that Jake wasn't going to die, for Mathias' sake. God, I couldn't even imagine the guilt that I would feel if Mathias had to spend the rest of his life in prison for standing up for me. I shivered as the thought entered my mind. Just then, there was a soft knock on the door. "Yeah?" Officer Dubois replied. The door slowly opened and another police officer peeked his head in, looked at Officer Dubois, and asked to speak with her privately for a moment. "Just a sec," she said to me, as she followed her co-worker out of the room. She had left the door open, just a tad, enough for me to see them talking in hushed voices. The guy officer had said something to Officer Dubois, which caused her to get a look of concern on her face. I tapped my foot nervously. *What is it that he can't say in front of me?* I wondered.

When Officer Dubois returned, a few seconds later, she still had a concerned look on her face. "Is everything alright?" I inquired. *Of course everything is not alright, Bliss,* I told myself, *why would you ask such a stupid question?* Officer Dubois looked down at her paperwork, as she shook her head and said, "It looks like he's going to live. He has suffered a lot of brain damage. Apparently he is in surgery now. The doctors expect him to live, but he will most likely be paralyzed from the neck down for the rest of his life. They say that he will be lucky if he is even able to talk ever again." "That's horrible," I gasped. "Well, the way I see it, the spoiled, rich, bastard got what was comin' to him. Those type of guys think everything and everyone is theirs for the takin', like they can do whatever the hell they want and their rich ass daddies will come waving money in people's faces and bail them out. This guy has a rap sheet a mile long, so I don't think we'll be keepin' your friend locked up for too long, but you didn't hear that from me," she said in a hushed tone. *Did I just hear that right?* I wondered. *Does that mean Mathias won't be in trouble?*

Officer Dubois continued asking me the details of that night. Once I had left no rock unturned and nothing to question, she said, "Oh, by the way, in case you were wonderin', your attacker's full name is,

Jacob Daniel Devereaux, Jr." A tinge of fear surged through my body. *Jacob Daniel Devereaux, Jr? That means that his father is Jacob Devereaux, my father's old business partner. The one that Neely had sent the fake ass fax to, the day after I had killed my father.* "You alright, girl?" Officer Dubois asked, "You look like you just saw the ghost of Marie Laveau, or somethin'." I took a deep breath and nodded, "Yeah, it's just been one hell of a night," I assured. "Yep, you've been put through the ringer," she agreed.

As I followed Officer Dubois out of the seclusion and solace of the room, and into the chaos of the station, I was hoping that Jake's father had never suspected the real reason for my father's sudden disappearance. If he had, this would be the perfect time for him to get revenge. I didn't know what all he had been told about everything that had happened within the previous couple of hours, but I was sure that my name would come up once he spoke with the police. Hell, I was pressing charges against his son, who, best case scenario, would be paralyzed for the rest of his life. *Shit,* I thought, *Mr. Devereaux will probably contact my mother to try to charm her into convincing me to drop the charges, then she will be able to find me and Neely!* We were almost at the door that led to the lobby, when I exclaimed, "I've changed my mind! I don't want to press charges against Jacob Devereaux, Jr!" Officer Dubois turned around and looked at me with a look of shock and surprise. "Miss Fontaine, I assure you that no harm will come to you for pressing charges, if that's what you are worried about. If you decide not to press charges, there will be no justice served. An alleged rapist will go without punishment. I urge you to reconsider," she pleaded. Every ounce of my being was angry with Jake for what he had done. Yes, I felt sorry for him for what had happened to him, that he probably would never walk again and all. But, deep down inside, I wanted him to suffer for his actions, for the damage that he had caused. I would never wish paralysis on anyone, I didn't want him to suffer like that. I wanted him to suffer in the courtroom. I wanted him to serve some jail time for the pain that he had caused me. I so badly wanted to press charges against him and stand up for myself and for every girl or woman who had been raped, and who had never gotten justice served. I wanted to, but I knew that I couldn't. I had to think of my safety, as well as Neely's safety. "No, I don't want to press charges." I stated. "Okay then, I can't force you to make the right decision. I will throw this file out, then," she promised, as she pushed a button, to unlock the door. I knew that once I stepped through the door and into the lobby, that was it. Jake would have no record of being a rapist. It was unfair and unjust, but necessary for our well-being and survival. I didn't need Cecily Fontaine catching wind of it, and coming in and wrecking the great life that I had built within the past couple of months. It may have been a selfish move, but I didn't care. Sometimes you just have to be selfish. Sometimes you have to put yourself and your well being first, because no one else will. I knew, right then and there, that it was a moment that I would revisit in my mind for years to come. The moment that I made a decision, a decision that I would not allow my over-analytical mind to criticize.

I had to do what I had to do. I didn't know what would happen to Mathias without my account of the rape, which caused Mathias' beat down of Jake. I didn't want to think about the fact that it could mean jail time for Mathias. I knew the harsh reality of the situation at hand, but I wasn't willing to risk my most treasured commodity, my freedom from my mother. I knew that momma would surely kill me dead, were she to ever see my face again. I had to keep my name as far away from her social circle as possible. As far as I knew, momma had not spoken to Jacob Devereaux since my father's disappearance, but you can never be too careful. Jacob Devereaux knew where my mother lived and he probably still had the house phone number, which hadn't changed. If he heard that Bliss Fontaine was accusing his son of rape, he would surely contact my mother in order to sort things out, like the hoity toity crowd are accustomed to doing. They will do anything to keep their family's name out of the media, unless it's on the news for some sort of self promotion, or some shit like that. I knew that Jake deserved to be punished for his actions, but I couldn't let my need for wrath destroy my future.

I reluctantly stepped through the doorway, into the lobby and shrugged my shoulders as I turned back and looked at the disappointed face of Officer Dubois. I felt like I was failing her. I felt like I was failing Mathias. I felt like I was failing Miss Dahlia. I felt like I was failing every woman who had ever been raped. I couldn't bear to look at Miss Dahlia. I knew that she was counting on me and I was letting her down. I hated it, but I knew that at that moment, I had to do the right thing for me and for Neely.

Chapter Twenty-Two

Mathias ended up being charged with Simple Assault Misdemeanor, because he did not have a weapon at the time of the fight. He served only ninety days in jail and had to pay a fine of two hundred dollars, which I insisted upon paying, with my own money. My burlesque career came to a screeching halt, due to the fact that I was now afraid of encountering another asshole like Jake. Thankfully, Miss Dahlia let me work at her shop. She had taken it upon herself to begin teaching me how to use my third eye. Neely and her went on and on about how I was catching on so quickly, I was a natural, they said. Miss Dahlia promised that I could begin taking on clients for readings once my intuition got a bit stronger. She taught me all about my Clair Senses; Clairvoyance, Clairaudience, Clairsentience, Clairscent, Clairtangency, Clairgustance, and Clairempathy. I would never admit this to Miss Dahlia, but it was all a bit overwhelming. Don't get me wrong, I loved learning about that kind of stuff, especially from someone as experienced as Dahlia, but it was a lot to learn and extremely draining. I welcomed the lessons, as they made the days spent without Mathias pass quickly.

September came and I began a new chapter of my life as a bonafide college student. I honestly can say that, growing up, I never thought that I would have the chance to go to college. I knew that Cecily Fontaine would rather eat dog shit that had been sitting in the sun, than see her daughter succeed in life. Starting college was somewhat bittersweet, as Mathias wasn't able to start his semester at LSU. Dahlia assured me that she had met with the LSU administration and that, due to the circumstances that caused Mathias to be locked up for the majority of the semester, they were going to allow him to come back in the spring. "Don't worry 'bout Thi, honey," Dahlia would say, "he's gonna be just fine. He'll be out before Thanksgivin', then they gonna let him start up classes in the spring. He can make up his lost semester next summer. Don't you worry, girl." I was beyond thankful that Dahlia and Mathias didn't hold anything against me. When I had fessed up to Dahlia and Neely about not pressing charges against that jerk, Jake, I had expected Dahlia to go bat shit crazy on me, and Neely to back her up all the way. To my surprise, they both agreed that I had made a smart decision, considering who Jake's daddy was. "We don't need yo' whole life gettin' wrecked because some rich ass frat boy can't keep his dang pinker in his pants. I'm tellin' ya girl, I can see it, you're gonna have a big life. Ya made the right decision. I know that Mathias will agree when I tell him," Dahlia had stated. Of course, Neely had to add her two cents too, saying, "Damn right, she made the right decision. I ain't 'bout to have our asses hauled back to Miss Cecily's house, hell nah! That crazy bitch would have a hay day torturin' our asses. Good thinkin', baby girl. Thank ya for thinkin' of us." I was shocked by their reactions, but hey, who was I to turn down accolades?

Miss Dahlia visited Mathias at least three times a week, while he was in jail. I didn't have the nerve to go up there until she had assured me that he had no hard feelings towards me. It was a Sunday afternoon in October, about halfway through his three month sentence. Mathias was happy to see me, although I could sense that he was worried about something. My senses told me that it had something to do with Jennifer. Miss Dahlia hadn't mentioned her since the traumatic night that caused Thi's lockup, but I had a gnawing feeling that things weren't going well between them. After we talked with Mathias for awhile, my intuition was validated. Mathias asked Dahlia if Jennifer had called. When Dahlia replied that she hadn't he mumbled, "yeah, I figured." Dahlia, trying to keep Mathias' spirits up told him that he didn't need to worry about it, that she would come around eventually. Mathias looked down and replied, "no, I don't think so, momma. I wrote Jen a few letters, tryin' to see if she'd come up here. I just didn't want her to think I'm some bad guy, ya know? I wanted her to see, that I'm still me, I wanted her to know that I haven't changed. She wrote me back a few days ago. She said it was over between us. She's moved on. Oh well, I guess it's for the best," he said as he moved his gaze from the floor, locking eyes with me. I knew that I shouldn't, but I had to say it, "She was never right for you to begin with. She's not soulful enough. That's a bitch move to give up on someone like that. Doesn't she realize how lucky she was? Does she even know how amazing you are? No, she doesn't, but I do. Thank you Mathias, for what you did for me. Thank you for caring about what happened to me. That's why you did it, right? You did it because you care about me, don't you?"

As the words flew out of my mouth, I braced myself for a letdown. I was all the way out on a skinny ass limb, and I knew it. Mathias didn't take his eyes off of me. He sat there and continued to stare into my eyes, I felt like he was trying to see my soul. An exhilarating tingle surged through my body. He took a deep breath, leaned forward, and whispered, "Bliss, I don't care about you." My body went numb, I felt like the wind had been knocked out of me. I wanted to get up and leave. I wanted to get as far away as I could from the humiliation and heartbreak that I was feeling. I wanted to run as fast as I could, far away from the boy that I longed for, the one who had strangled my heart, as well as my confidence. I wanted to bolt, but I couldn't. I couldn't move. I felt like one of the people who paint themselves and stand stoically still, hoping for a tip from a tourist in Jackson Square. I wanted to leave, but I couldn't. I'm grateful for my temporary catatonic state, for without it, I wouldn't have heard Mathias finish, by saying, "I don't *just* care about you. Bliss, I *love* you."

www.ingramcontent.com/pod-product-compliance
Lightning Source LLC
Chambersburg PA
CBHW071918220626
47052CB00002B/401